OCTOBER RAIN

J. W. Dunn

Trenton, Georgia

Print ISBN: 978-1-958891-02-5
Ebook ISBN: 979-8-88531-594-4

Published by BookLocker.com, Inc., Trenton, Georgia.

Printed on acid-free paper.

The characters and events in this book are fictitious. Any similarity to real persons, living or dead, is coincidental and not intended by the author.

BookLocker.com, Inc.
2023

First Edition

Library of Congress Cataloguing in Publication Data
Dunn, J. W.
OCTOBER RAIN by J. W. Dunn
Library of Congress Control Number: 2023918422

ACKNOWLEDGEMENT

The "Hog Hunter" party game description and song lyrics are adapted from the "Hog Drover" game which appears on pp. 810-11 in A Treasury of American Folklore, edited by B. A. Botkin and published in New York by Crown Publishers, Inc., 1944.

Basically, we need to recognize that man cannot walk in a straight line or otherwise maintain a directional course without relying on some tangible clue wholly apart from his own instincts.

The Wilderness Route Finder
-Calvin Rutstrum

For Palmyra

October Rain is a work of fiction. All similarities between actual persons, living or dead and actual places and events are purely coincidental.

OCTOBER RAIN

J. W. Dunn

PART I

Chapter One

February 5, 1906

"For crying out loud, Ma, I think you're putting too much stock in the slur of a dirty-mouthed little boy," Maud said and stepped from the china safe to the kitchen table. Plates clacked and thumped as she and Sarah set the table for supper.

Retty stood in the heat of the cookstove holding a wooden spoon. With the back of her wrist, she pushed a graying strand of auburn hair from her forehead. Her blue eyes fixed on Maud. After almost twenty-four years of marriage and six children, but for an occasional backache, she felt as spry as she did on the evening she first laid eyes on Thurston Knox.

"Maybe so, honey," Retty said. "But that dirty-mouthed little boy is Joe Burgess's own little brother and you're to keep your distance from Mr. Joseph Burgess 'til I get to the bottom of this. Find out what it's all about before your pa catches wind of it."

On their knees in a far corner of the kitchen-house, Asa and Callie rolled an empty thread spool back and forth between them. Asa looked up suddenly and gripped the spool in his fist.

They were talking about it again, about yesterday at church. His fight with that hatchet-faced, snot-nosed bully down by the spring.

"Back to me, Asa," Callie said and clapped her hands.

"Play with her, Asa," Sarah said, and he rolled the spool to Callie.

"Go ahead and light the lamp, Sarah. It's beginning to get dark in here," Retty said and resented the sudden doubt and confusion that rushed her thoughts. Her ma had objected to her marrying Thurston.

"He's nothing," she'd said. "His ma's some kind of Indian or Lord knows what all. I expect better for my girls. I want more for my daughters," she'd said. And from the day Retty married Thurston until the day she died, her ma never really smiled at her again. Anytime Retty looked at her, her ma's eyes sank into sadness and disappointment.

She glanced at Maud. She knew how it felt to be in love, heart pounding, hands shaking, needing to share in love, only to find that your ma didn't approve of your beau, didn't think him so handsome, ambitious or such a fine catch. Thinking about it now, Retty wasn't so sure she had really loved Thurston from the moment she first laid eyes on him the night of the dance at her pa's house. Swinging round the dance floor, she glanced up and saw him leaning against the doorjamb, his hat set at a jaunty angle across his face, watching the frolic like he was the one giving the party for his friends and neighbors.

But my concern with Joe Burgess is different from Ma's objection to Thurston. I'm not worried about Joe's blood or how much land his pa farms, Retty thought. *His folks are faithful church members, but I'm gonna find out what all this loose talk is before I allow anymore of Joe's courting Maud. Besides, Thurston has been out of sorts of late, not quite himself, and it won't do to have him upset about Maud and her beau.*

Chapter Two

Thurston Knox's eighty acres lay on the west side of the Hennessey Creek and the Buskin Road. The road followed the crest of a pine ridge that wandered from south to north ranging a mile to three miles west of the creek. As the road approached the Knox house from the south, a short lane forked left to the front gate in a picket fence that enclosed the house and yard. The road continued north skirting the picket fence and passed a second gate at the side of the house, a kitchen-house, a log smokehouse, and a barn. The board and batten walls of the main house, the kitchen-house and the barn had weathered to a silver-gray. A four foot wide by six foot long walk made of two by six boards spanned the gap between the back porch of the main house and the kitchen-house. The main house and outbuildings were roofed with cypress board shingles.

In the failing daylight, Luke Knox rode a brown and white pinto horse from the north toward the barn. With his hat pulled low over his eyes, he sat easy in the saddle and balanced a double bit ax across the saddle bow. A lone calf inside the barn lot followed along the board fence, and he knew his pa was in the barn at the evening milking. Woodsmoke drifted from the kitchen-house stovepipe and hung in the February chill.

"Whoa, Button," he said and tugged the reins. He swung from the saddle and raising the ax in one hand, he drove the bit into a chopping block near the fence. He unlatched the gate and led the horse into the lot. The calf edged against his leg. He pushed it away with a gentle nudge of the knee, latched the gate and walked Button toward the barn, the calf following.

Hired man back from chores. Hired man, but no wages. Durn him.

Iron hinges squalled as Luke pulled open the barn door and led the horse into the hay dust and corn-fed effluvium. In the jaundiced light,

Thurston straightened on the milking stool, craned his neck to see over the ridge of the cow's back, and wiped his palm over his pepper-gray mustache. He felt certain he was dying, but he had told nobody; nobody else knew.

"Mind you don't let the calf in, son." Thurston said thinking, *Luke's a good boy, hardworking.* "Did you chop down plenty of green fodder?" He had sent him to chop down holly saplings to feed their woods stock in the late winter poverty.

"Yes sir, Pa," he said. Square-framed but already taller by an inch than his pa, he talked over the saddle as he hung the stirrup iron on the pommel and loosened the cinch. "I went clear up the ridge nigh to Matt's turnoff lane." He pulled the saddle and blanket from the horse. "There's still plenty of acorn mast."

"I know there is, son, but them cows need some green browse. They're apt to founder on too many acorns. Did you happen across Matt Tarroll while you was up there?"

"No, sir, not hide nor hair of him," he said. "Steady, Button." Luke moved with the even rhythm of habit, without haste, but without sloth and swung the saddle astride a hickory pole nailed catty-corner in the near end of the barn and draped the blanket over the saddle. And he knew he was going to have to say it again. *Hard-headed old goat.* Taking up the bridle reins, he walked the horse down the barn hall beyond the mules' stalls and the corncrib.

For a moment, Thurston watched Luke. He had thought of talking to Matt Tarroll about his condition, but on mulling it over, he grew dubious about the idea. Matt Tarroll was Retty's younger brother, and he might, without intending, let it slip to her. It wouldn't do to have her upset when there was nothing to be done. He bent over, and pressing his head against the barrel of the cow's belly, he sopped a washrag in a pail of warm water and gently rinsed the milk-tight udder and teats. His ears piqued at the faint click of teeth on steel bit as Luke slipped the bridle off Button's head. The sound of finality, the end of the day sound of promised rest. He believed everything was in God's hand, but he felt he had to fix things for Retty and the young'uns the best he could, make it easier for them after he was gone. He wanted to break new ground and plant ten more acres of cotton come spring if God granted him the time. It would mean an extra year's cash for Retty and the young'uns. They wouldn't want after he was gone. As for himself, he'd been ready for a while. He married Retty one month and was baptized within the year. *Washed in the blood of the Lamb*. She just wouldn't let him rest until he joined the church, and he was glad for it.

The cow restively shifted her weight from one hind foot to the other.

"Sah, Penny," Thurston said.

Seth, their oldest, had left home a couple of years ago to make his own way and since had married. Always dependable, even tempered; Luke, nigh on to grown, still lived at home, but of late, he'd been raring to go on his own. Thurston knew he ought to set the boy free, but he needed his help to raise ten more acres of cotton one more season. Maud was sixteen. She was sweet on Joe Burgess, and Joe had been prompt and serious in his courting. They would be married by this time next year. Still, that left Retty with the three youngest. She could hardly fare on her own with three young'uns to provide for, could hardly make it without Luke's help. He had to find the right words to keep him working on the place for one more crop.

The stall door banged shut, and Luke shuffled back along the dark barn hall. He cut his eyes at his pa's back and unlatched the corncrib door. He stepped inside and pushing his hat to the back of his head, he squatted on his heels. A gray striped cat came to its feet in a dark corner, yawned, bowed its back in a stiff-legged arch, and stretched on its forepaws then, sat on its haunches, and with half-closed, yellow eyes, watched Luke pick among the corn.

I'm gonna have to raise it again. Have to say it all over again. Confound it all, even he knows that he can't keep me here forever, Luke thought as the pale brown, dry corn shucks rattled and whispered in his hands.

Picking up one ear of corn, he tossed it back onto the pile, then another. Finally, he chose four that looked no different from any of the ears he had culled. He pushed three of them into one of the oversized pockets of his denim coat, and holding the last ear, he rose and stepped from the corncrib.

"Me and you and your Uncle Morgan are set to gather over to your grandpa's place in the morning to mark and castrate pigs," Thurston said. "You recall me telling you that, don't you?" He bent, dipped the sop rag into the pail, and again, wiped the cow's teats and udder.

"Yes sir," he said, wondering how he would ever have anything that was his own if he wasn't his own man. He was old enough. *Hard-headed!*

He leaned against the outside post of the milking stall, and his shoulder brushed his pa's hat from the nail where he always hung it when he milked. Luke stooped and picked up the hat and dusted it against his leg.

"Be particular, Luke," Thurston said. "You'll knock trash in the milking pail."

"Yes sir," he said. He hung the hat on the nail and stepped to the middle of the barn hall and stood, his legs astride, eyes fixed on the back of his pa's weather faded blue coat as he slowly parted the pale, dry shucks at the silk end of the ear. He opened his mouth, started to speak, hesitated, and tore open the ear of corn, folding the shucks back over the stem end of the cob.

"I figure it's time you let me go on my own, Pa." Luke's words rushed, his voice a pitch higher than normal, and the tense sound of his voice angered him. He felt his face burn as he pushed the shucked ear into an empty pocket, then pulled another ear from the opposite pocket.

Aware that Luke had raised the troublesome question again, Thurston busied himself, trying to think of what he should say, how he should say it and wrung water from the washrag and hung it from the edge of the feed trough. Swishing the leftover rinse water inside the pail, he glanced up at Luke then dashed the water into the corner of the stall. He set the rinse pail to one side, and leaning forward, he pressed his cheek against the cow's warm side and set the milking pail beneath her teats.

"I gotta have you to help me out on the place, Luke," Thurston said.

"I don't see how come, Pa," Luke said. The terse edge faded from his voice, and he relaxed, having broached the subject of going on his own. He ripped the shucks opening another ear of corn, his hands and fingers working with habit, without thought.

"I just don't see how I can get on without you, yet, son," Thurston said. "Maybe in the fall after picking time, but I'm sure to need you 'til then." He bent to the milking, and squeezing a teat in first one hand then the other, needles of milk sang in the bottom of the pail.

"With Seth gone and married, it's just me and you to break the new ground and make a crop," he said. Foam began to head in the milking pail. "The girls help, too, but Asa ain't but ten years old and won't be any real help to me for a couple more years."

"Yes sir, I know it, Pa. But I'm gonna be nineteen, come October," he said, thinking, *What did Asa's being but ten years old have to do with him going on his own? When Seth asked to go on his own, his pa just shook his hand and told him to walk upright and always remember who he was.*

Luke stepped into the first mule's stall then the other's and dropped an ear of corn into each trough. Going into Button's stall, he slapped the horse's rounded rump and edged between him and the wall.

When he freed Seth, he didn't say, "Luke ain't but sixteen years old," or how old Asa was or if the girls helped, too, or anybody else. Rubbing Button's cheek, he let him take the ear of corn from his hand, the wet breath hot in his palm.

"I don't think it's fair for you to expect me to stay here till Asa's big enough to do a man's work," he said. Button and the mules slowly crunched the corn, and milk ripped into the foam head in the milking pail.

Coming from the stall, Luke latched the gate and smeared the horse slobber from his hand onto his britches leg and pulled the last ear of corn from his coat pocket. He edged around his pa's bent back, ducked his head under an unlit lantern hanging from a ceiling joist, and stood at the cow's feed trough.

"When Seth was my age, you'd done freed him," Luke said, his voice grating like a file on hardened steel, "and he was planning on getting married."

As he twisted the ear of corn in his tightened palms, yellow, blue and red kernels shelled from the cob, spilled through his fingers and pecked the bottom of the trough. The cow muzzled the grains from the smooth wood, and needles of milk ripped the rising froth in the pail.

Thurston knew it wasn't fair, but he didn't see how he could let Luke go. Seth had married a year ago, and he and his wife settled on forty acres on the other side of the Hennessey Creek. The day after Christmas, their baby was born; a son just five years and four months younger than Callie, his and Retty's youngest. Thurston turned his head and laying his cold cheek against the cow's warm side, he looked up at Luke.

"Is that it, Luke?" he said, still milking. "You're looking to get yourself married?"

"No, sir, I ain't lookin to get married, Pa." He stepped around his pa and tossed the gleaned cob down the barn bay toward the door. Shuck wings fluttered as the corncob wheeled across the dying light. "How could I be looking to get married and I ain't even my own man yet? I just want a chance to work for me."

Agitated, tired, and afraid, Thurston pushed his head against the cow's ribs. The cow shifted her hind feet.

"Sah, cow," Thurston said. "Just where do you aim on getting work this time of year, Luke?"

"I figured I could work for Seth for starters," Luke said.

"For Seth? Have y'all talked about this? Has he promised you work?"

"No, sir, I ain't said nothing to Seth, but I figure he'd give me work."

Thurston let go of the cow's teats, sat up straight on the stool, and craned his neck so he could see over the cow's back and look Luke in the eye. He wiped his palm across his mustache, Luke staring back at him. Thurston thought about what he should say, how to explain to a boy, a young man, who wanted to be free, deserved to be free and on his own, that he needed him to stay and help him, how to tell him that he was tired, and he was the sole support of a woman and four young'uns, and that he was afraid because he had been tired of late, afraid that somewhere deep inside he was sick because he couldn't get rested? How to tell him all this without telling him that he was afraid? Say it without begging, without anger?

"I just don't see how I can make it without you right now, Luke, and what I hear you saying is you wanna help support Seth's household and leave me and your ma and the young'uns go. Is that it?"

"That ain't what I'm saying, and it ain't what I meant, Pa."

"Looks to me like Seth's gonna have a tough enough time making ends meet as it is with Martha and the baby, let alone paying extra for day help." Thurston struggled to keep his voice steady, reasonable.

"All I'm saying, Pa, is 'Don't tie the ox that pulls the mill.'"

Luke's words, twisted and contrary, rattled in Thurston's ears. He tried to sort them out, tried to make sense of them, but it was more than he could handle.

"Don't you try and spout Scripture at me, boy," Thurston said. "Your ma gave you birth and gave you suck, and every morsel of meat and bread you ever ate, we put in your mouth. Now, I ain't gonna set here and let you twist and bend the Scriptures against me like I'm some kinda heathen and none the wiser."

Luke turned and walked toward the pale dusk hovering outside the barn door.

"I ain't so sure who the heathen on this place is," he said.

"Say?" Thurston said. "Say? What did you say, boy?"

He'd plainly heard Luke's words, but he wanted to make him look him in the eye and say it. Say it to his face. He stood, overturning the milking stool. Luke broke and ran through the open barn door into the dying daylight. Thurston followed, square-framed, his back holding the slight stoop of his milking posture. He reached the door as Luke climbed the lot gate.

"What's that you say, boy?" Thurston said. Fear welled in his chest, palpable, and rising, it tightened in his throat.

"I said, 'I ain't so sure who the heathen on this place is!'" Luke stood outside the fence in the Buskin Road. "And I ain't gonna hang around here to find out who is neither." He pushed his hands into his pockets, hunched his shoulders, and turned north up the road, his stride, defiant and certain.

Thurston reached the lot gate and gripping the top board with both hands, he leaned forward and watched Luke trudge up the road. He'd gone and done what he feared he would do, but he couldn't set him free, couldn't agree to let him go. He needed his help on the place for one more year, for one more crop, another ten acres.

Luke rounded the near bend in the Buskin Road, and Thurston caught brief glimpses of him between the trunks of the tall, straight pines then he was gone. Slowly, he straightened from the gate, and taking his left hand in his right, with the tip of his forefinger, he traced a fishhook-shaped scar that curved round his left fore-knuckle. He turned and ambled back into the cavernous barn. Somewhere in the gloom, a mule in half-slumber, dreaming warm days of gnats and flies, stomped the packed dirt floor. Thurston breathed deeply, heaved a sigh through his nose that rustled the hairs of his mustache, and thought how pleasant it would be to curl up in the back of one of the stalls and go to sleep. Pinching the crown of his hat, he lifted it from its nail, set it on his head, and slapped the cow on the flat of her rump.

"Sah, Penny," he said.

He stooped and picked up the milking pail. The cow swung her head around and looked at him, ball-eyed, ruminating, slobber dripping from her jaws. He pulled the slipknot on the lead rope around her horns and walked her through the barndoor into the lot and loosed her from the rope. The cow made one mournful, plaintive low, and her calf trotted to her and nuzzled her warm udder and teats. He went out the gate and latched it, and once more before turning toward the house, he looked beyond the cow and calf, across the barn lot, up the Buskin Road that curved into the failing light.

“Confounded boy.” Shaking his head, he hung the coiled lead rope over the gatepost and walked to the kitchen-house.

Chapter Three

"I see Pa coming from the barn," Sarah said.

Retty looked at her and wiped her upper lip with the hem of her apron.

"Bring the old yellow flowered serving bowl from the safe, honey, and help me take up the peas."

"Yes, ma'am."

Retty folded a dishtowel, and with it, she lifted the lid from the iron pot. Steam rolled into the warm, yellow light, and she ladled the black-eyed peas and a ham hock into the bowl. Turning to the table, Sarah set the bowl next to the lighted lamp.

Placing drinking glasses at each plate, Maud said, "You might as well get the milk, Sarah."

"You want clabber or sweet-milk, Ma?" Sarah said.

"I think I'll take sweet-milk, honey," Retty said.

"I want clabber," Asa said, looking up from his corner, the spool clutched in his fist.

"Me, too," said Callie.

"You young'uns will drink what's on the table," Maud said as Sarah went to the kitchen shelf for the milk pitcher.

The back door abruptly opened, and Thurston stepped into the kitchen. He shut the door against the evening chill and for a moment savored the supper-warmth against his cold cheek. He set the rinse pail on the floor and the milking pail on the kitchen shelf and removing his hat he hung it on a nail on the inside of the door and blew his breath into his cupped hands.

"Pa!" Callie said. She scrambled to her feet and ran to him.

His gloom lightened at the sight of Callie and the sound of her voice. *Sunshine,* he thought. *Sweet as syrup.*

Asa glared into his pa's dark face but lowered his head when Thurston glanced at him.

Asa. Feisty as a colt. Quick tempered. Takes a strong rein hand.

"Pa," Callie said as Thurston picked her up. "Maud said I can't have no clapper for supper."

"I think we can find a glass of clabber for Pa's baby girl," Thurston said. He pressed his lips and mustache to her cheek and kissed her.

"Your 'taches is cold, Pa!" Callie said, shrugging her shoulder to the kissed cheek.

"It's getting mighty cold outside, sugar," he said. He watched Retty pull a platter of baked sweet potatoes from the warmer over the stove and set it on the table.

"Maud," he said. "You and Sarah take the young'uns over in the house and put another stick of wood in the fireplace." He lowered Callie to the floor. "You go with Maud, sugar."

Maud watched her pa as he peeled off his coat and hung it next to his hat, Maud thinking, *What has Luke gone and told him about what Joe's dirty-mouthed little brother said?* Sarah set the milk pitcher on the table, leaving three glasses to be filled.

"Callie" Maud said. "You and Asa c'mon and help me and Sarah."

"Don't run in the house, Asa," Retty said.

"Yessum," Asa said.

He and Callie slipped through the door ahead of Sarah and Maud, and Asa dashed across the walk to the back porch.

"Ma said don't run in the house, Asa," Sarah said.

"I ain't in the house yet."

"It's just the same as."

"Ain't dunnit."

Callie bounced on her tiptoes. "It's cold out here."

"Get in by the fireplace, sugar," Sarah said.

Asa ran into the big front room ahead of the girls and picked up a stick of firewood and dropped it on the glowing, pulsing embers in the fireplace. Fiery sparks showered up the clay chimney. He stepped back thinking how his pa had switched him because he licked that bastard and bloodied his nose and then, he, the snot-nosed bully, sat down right in the middle of the congregation, and him a bastard, to boot.

"Asa, be careful with that fire," Maud said.

*

With his back to Retty, Thurston leaned so as not to block the light from the lamp and carefully poured the fresh milk into a large crock.

"Is ole Penny still giving plenny milk, Thurston?" Retty said. She stood between the table and stove listening to the milk pour into the bowl.

"Yeah, she's giving plenny," he said. "But as cold as it is, I left a little more than usual for the calf."

Frowning, Retty pressed her curled forefinger to her pursed lips. When he sent the young'uns from the kitchen, she figured something was amiss, something more than whether the cow was still giving milk or not, something the telling of which wouldn't wait until they were alone in bed.

Does he know about what Joe Burgess's little brother said? Did Luke hear idle talk and tell him and he's been mulling over how to handle it? Whatever it was, she knew he wouldn't say until he sorted it out for himself.

He pulled out a drawer under the kitchen shelf and picked through it until he found a clean flour sack cloth and a piece of sacking twine. He covered the milk with the cloth and wrapped the twine around the cloth and the top of the crock, thinking about the spell that had gripped him last September during cotton picking when he heaved a full cotton sack into the wagon bed. His vision had blurred, and the white-hot air took on a rosy hue. He'd staggered and clutched the wagon sideboards and hung on until he caught his balance and his vision cleared then looked into the field to see if Retty or any of the young'uns had noticed. None had seen, and tentatively, fearful of fainting, he emptied his cotton sack and returned to the field. By dusk, he was burnt out, but the only pain he felt was in his fingertips, which the sharp, brittle points of the cotton hulls had pricked and scratched raw. He dismissed the spell as too much sun, too much bending and lifting, nothing a night's sleep wouldn't allay, and he hadn't mentioned it to Retty. But the next morning, a weakness bound his arms and shoulders, and he remembered that Retty's pa, Mr. Rufe Tarroll, had a couple of fainting spells before his heart finally gave out.

"Well, Retty," he said, tying the twine around the cloth cover over the crock with a slipknot, "Luke's up and gone." He didn't turn around.

He couldn't look her in the eye. Ashamed? But he didn't know what he had done to be ashamed.

"What'd you mean, Thurston?" she said. She wiped her hands on her apron, watching him, feeling her shoulders growing lax and knew that what bothered him didn't concern Maud and Joe Burgess but Luke. "What d'you mean, 'up and gone?'"

"He commenced on me again about freeing him," Thurston said. He spread his hands toward the heat of the stove. "I told him that I didn't see how I could let him go now, that we got too much work to do between now and pickin' time."

"Hmm," Retty said. She didn't quite know what to say. He had acted downright strange, overbearing, ever since Luke first mentioned going on his own. Luke ought not to have left without his pa's blessing, but it wasn't like Thurston to not allow an older son his independence. Seth's leave-taking was no more than a handshake, and an admonition to walk morally upright, as it should be.

"Luke seems to be of a mind that somehow he can work for Seth and that somehow Seth can pay him."

"You know Seth ain't got nothing to offer Luke."

"I know it and told him so, but he commenced to chide with me, and when I wouldn't allow it, he lit out up the Buskin Road."

"Headed for Seth's place?" she said and turned to the stove. With her dishtowel, she gripped the oven door handle and swung it open. Heat enveloped her throat and face, and she felt the roots of her hair pull her scalp. She reached into the oven, pressed the top of the browned corn bread pone with her fingertips, and quickly withdrew her hand. The bread rose back to shape, and with the dishtowel, she pulled the pan from the oven, and set it on the stove top.

"I reckon," he said. "I don't know where else he'd go expecting to be taken in after running away."

He'd been determined to say the right words to Luke, reasonable words, words to convince, yet somehow, the right words had eluded him, slipped from his grasp, and he couldn't figure out how they were lost.

"He'll have to cross the Hennessey swamp to get to Seth's place," she said. "He's apt to get turned around in the dark."

"No, he won't get lost. He'll take the cutoff trail past Matt's place. The only crossing on the creek for a coupla miles either way is on that trail," Thurston said. "But Seth knows I ain't freed Luke, and he won't give him work even if he had the money to pay him. Not without talking to me first anyhow."

She watched him in silence as he rubbed the fishhook-shaped scar on his left fore-knuckle and stared at the stove. Again, he extended his hands toward the heat.

"You may as well set the cornbread on the table, Retty and call the young'uns. I'm gonna have to get up early and ride over to Pa's in the morning and help him mark his shoats."

The kitchen suddenly felt hot, and he took a deep breath and sighed. He pressed his mustache with his warm palm.

"No, Seth'll feed him supper over there tonight," he said. "He'll fetch him home tomorrow or day after tomorrow. Saturday, sure."

Chapter Four

Pulling his hands from his coat pockets, Luke fastened his collar button and tugged his hat brim down closer to his ears.

"Durn him!" His words spouted a fierce vapor into the cold dusk. He breathed into his cupped palms, rubbed them together then thrust his fists into his coat pockets again. The cold gripped his shoulders and neck, and in the dying light, he saw a lone brown thrasher scratching among the dry leaves under the hawthorn and huckleberry bushes that overhung the road ditch.

He figured he'd head for Seth's place on the far side of Hennessey Creek, but the moon wasn't going to rise until late, so he wouldn't be able to see his way through the dark woods for several hours. He had often hunted and trapped in these woods, during daylight and at night, sometimes alone but usually with Seth and their ma's younger brother, Matt Tarroll. Matt was four years older than him and only a year older than Seth, and they had worked and played and fished and hunted together since Luke could remember, and he felt at home in the pine woods that covered the ridge along which the Buskin Road curved and in the three- to six-mile-wide flat woods, which they called a swamp that lay on either side of Hennessey Creek. But every few years, a panther meandered through the countryside. Grandma Knox said the Hennessey swamp was part of the panther's hunting grounds, and folks had heard it scream and seen signs of it, off and on, for years. Luke had heard it scream, too.

In his right pocket, his hand curled round his Barlow pocketknife, and in his left pocket, he pinched a kernel of corn between his forefinger and thumb. He pulled the kernel from his pocket and held it in front of his eyes, hardly seeing it in the fading light. He slipped it into his mouth.

A couple of years before Matt or Seth got married, Matt bought a house place and eighty acres from Uncle Doss and Aunt Mavis Tarroll the fall before he married Tillie. Uncle Doss was Matt's and his ma's older brother, and Aunt Mavis was his ma's oldest childhood friend. Aunt Mavis would say that she and Retty couldn't be sisters, so she married Doss, and their young'uns were cousins all the same. After cotton picking, Luke and Seth lived with Matt and helped him make repairs and changes on the house to make things handy for Tillie. One night they made a coon hunt in the swamp, and when the late fall night grew cold an hour or so before daybreak, they stopped on the high bank of the creek and built a fire. As they savored the heat and soaked in the communal warmth, a scream cut the darkness. A chill slid along Luke's spine, and the short hairs bristled on his nape. He drove his eyes into the darkness beyond the flickering light of their warming fire. Spit dried in his mouth, and the longer he stared, the more afraid he became to look away from the dark. No one spoke for a long moment.

"You hear that? That's a damn panther," Seth whispered, hoarse, his voice almost breaking. "He can't be more 'n a quarter mile back down the creek. You think he's trailing us, Matt?"

Luke looked at Seth, then at Matt. The roof of his mouth tasted sharp and acrid as a twenty-two cartridge brass. They stared at each other over the licking flames, breathless, wordless.

"Light that carbide lamp, Seth," Matt said.

"We're outta water," Seth said. "And I ain't going down to the creek to get more."

Matt's two hounds slunk out of the darkness, and Matt held his twenty-two rifle, the only gun they had, on each dog until he was certain each approaching shadow and sound was a dog. With their tails tucked between their legs and the hairs bristling along their spines, the hounds whined and sulked next to the fire.

"Sic the hounds... sic Soldier and Queenie on him, Matt," Seth whispered, and grabbing the two dogs by the scuff of their necks, he dragged them from the fire.

"Sic, Queenie! Sic Soldier! Hunt!" The hounds moaned and walled their eyes and refused to leave the men or the firelight.

"Drag in more wood," Matt whispered. "I'll keep my eyes peeled and rifle ready."

"That twenty-two ain't enough firepower to stop no panther," Seth said.

"Just hope it'll sting him enough to scare him off."

Tentatively, Seth and Luke ventured out and lugged in all the deadfall wood they could reach within the small circle of light cast by the fire. As the fire grew larger and pushed light farther into the dark, they gathered more wood. Matt kept his rifle handy, and they talked in hushed voices around the blaze peering into the dark until daylight, then walked home.

Over the next few weeks, up and down the Hennessey, anytime two or more folks gathered together, they talked of hearing it or seeing its tracks, or of finding a partially eaten calf or hog carcass hidden under leaves and twigs, but nobody ever saw the panther. It stalked the keen edge of every idle dread and tongue then, abruptly, it was gone, as silently and secretly as it had come.

*

Luke knew it'd be a shorter walk to cut across the swamp to the foot log over the creek beyond Matt's barn, but it would be easy for him to get turned around before the late moonrise, and it got light enough for him to see. The swamp was wooded by towering cypress, oak and hickory and bitter pecan trees and was clear of thick underbrush except for deadfall thickets that grew here and there where wind or ice had torn off large branches or toppled trees. Cross briars and switch cane and holly, and hawthorn shrubs laid claim to the full sunlight that flooded the storm breaks and each strove to choke out the other. Some of the thickets covered two, sometimes three acres, and Luke knew if he wandered into one of these, he'd likely have to wait until daylight to find his way out. The night was too cold to sleep on the ground without a quilt.

With his tongue, he worked the saliva-softened grain of corn between his jaw teeth and crushed it. The dry, sweet flavor brought more saliva, and he slowly chewed, figuring his best bet was to walk in on Matt's lane and pick up the cutoff trail beyond his barn. Wide enough to pass a wagon along much of its length, the foot trail meandered across the Hennessey swamp and struck the Salem Road about two miles above Seth's place.

Clenching his elbows against his sides, he slowly chewed and ground the corn kernel into a coarse paste and swallowed it. He thought about what he'd say to Seth. He figured his brother wasn't going to like his jumping the trace chains, and that he'd take their pa's part. He jammed his fists deeper into his pockets and hunched his shoulders. Wading in the darkness that flooded the road under the tall pines, he heard the muffled thump of his feet, regular as his heartbeat. The dead cold gave no sound now.

He thought, *I'll say, "Hell, Seth, I'm full-grown. I'll be nineteen years old come October, and you know how the old man is. He'll keep me in harness till Asa's full-grown, too, if he can."*

"Damn him. Hard-headed as a durn goat." And he grappled for the words of his explaining to Seth, wrangling to make him see that he was right, until he emerged from the shadow of the tall pines where the road skirted the west side of Matt Tarroll's cornfield. Under the failing daylight, last year's pale cornstalks slanted, brittle and tattered, and he made out the zigzag crawl of the split-rail fence that cornered at the junction of Matt's turnoff lane and the Buskin Road.

Matt and Seth were their own men, on their own, earning their own ways, making their own lives. But Luke was his pa's hired man. Envy gouged his gut like a stick hung in a chicken's craw.

But not now, by God. No more. I'm nobody's man but my own.

He heard a stirring of leaves in the bushes along the road ditch at his back, louder and heavier than the scratching of a bird. He stopped and stood stock-still. Gripping the Barlow in his pocket, he slowly turned and faced the road he had just walked. Motionless except for the rise and fall of his chest, he listened; his visible breath bloomed and faded. He was very cold. A small dark form ambled from the roadside scrub and with an unhurried, rolling gait, crossed the pale trace and vanished again into a stir and rustle of dry leaves.

"Coon," he said.

For a long time, he strained his eyes and ears against the dark silence until a breeze, cold as well water, licked his cheeks and rattled the leaves of last year's cornstalks in Matt's field. The smell of woodsmoke wafted on the air.

Abruptly, Luke turned and struck out down Matt's lane toward the tall cypress trees that grew along the Hennessey Creek. From a quarter mile distance, Luke saw the soft, yellow lamplight glowing in a window of Matt's house. A wide dogtrot hall with parlor and bedrooms on either side ran through the house from the front porch to the back porch. Behind the house, Uncle Doss had built a kitchen-house, a log smokehouse, and a chicken house of peeled pine poles, and farther out, a large barn of board and batten. When Uncle Doss caught Texas fever and offered to sell it to Matt, Luke's pa said it was worth the price just for the barn and acreage and rode into Clemson with Matt and helped him borrow the money at Hunter's Mercantile. First thing, Matt asked Seth and Luke to help him move the cookstove, china safe, and kitchen table from the kitchen-house into a back room in the main house. He said he wouldn't have his wife getting out of bed on cold mornings and walking a plank in the dark to fix breakfast. They all wondered if the notion was his or Tillie's, but they moved the kitchen into a back room of the main house and tore down the kitchen-house and used the boards to repair the barn and back porch flooring. Luke heard his pa tell his ma that it was Matt's business, but he thought it was foolishness to put a kitchen in the main house, where if they didn't burn the whole place down, it would heat the house up so in the summertime they wouldn't be able to find a cool place to sleep. But he never said it to Matt.

Chapter Five

Cold soaked through Luke's britches legs and coat, and the smell of woodsmoke and fried meat brought saliva to his mouth. He swallowed and picked up his pace down the sloping lane toward the lamp-lighted house. He savored the thought of backing to Tillie's cookstove and burning the cold from his pants and coat, eating a biscuit and a piece of fried meat, but as he neared the house, he decided not to knock at their door. Naturally, they'd want to know how come he was out so late, and he didn't want to explain things to them, not now, and anyhow, he figured Matt would say about the same things that Seth would, taking his pa's part.

Matt's hounds scrabbled from under the front porch and ran and barked along the inside of the picket fence.

"Here, Soldier. Here, Queenie." He softly called the dogs' names to quiet them, his voice visible in the cold twilight. Footfalls thumped the floor inside the house. The front door latch clicked, and the door swung open.

"Here, Soldier!" Matt called. "Hush!" Then he said, "Who's that in the lane?"

Luke decided on the spot that he'd say nothing to Matt and Tillie about his trouble. He'd say he was headed for Seth's place to give him a hand marking pigs in the morning. He'd say he'd as soon make the walk this evening after dark as he would in the morning before daylight.

"It's me, Matt," he said. "It's Luke!"

"Well, c'mon up to the house, Luke," Matt said. Bareheaded and in his shirtsleeves, Matt walked down the steps into the yard. "You know old Soldier and Queenie ain't gonna bite you."

Luke lifted the gate latch, and in the yard, he gripped Matt's hand.

"You ain't taken supper, yet, have you, old son?" Matt said and slapped Luke's shoulder.

"No, matter of fact, I ain't."

"C'mon in outta the cold and let's eat a bite," Matt said. "Tillie's just now set the table. I was just thinking how it'd be a good night to take the hounds out and see if they could tree a coon."

"I 'spect it is," Luke said. "I seen one cross the Buskin Road near the edge of your cornfield, and there's still plenny acorn mast on the ground." He doffed his hat, and unbuttoning his coat, he followed Matt across the porch into the house. At the far end of the dark hall, he saw light coming from the kitchen.

Durn! They'll wanna know how come I didn't ride Button.

"Tillie," Matt said. "Luke's here. Lay another place. Looks like the coon hunt's on tonight."

"Evening, Luke," she said. Rising from the table, she smiled and smoothed her skirt and apron. Her sleeves were rolled to her elbows. Matt pulled out his chair and sat down.

"Evening, Tillie," Luke said. Surprised at how pretty she looked, he gazed, almost stared, her eyes smiling back at him. Her face held a light blush in the kitchen heat, and the lamplight softened her hair and darkened her brown eyes.

"You're just in time for supper, such as it is," she said. "Hang your hat and coat and wash up." Stepping to the china safe, she took down another plate, knife and fork and leaning across the table, she set his place on Matt's right. The light caught the sheen of down on her arms then spread over platters of biscuits, baked sweet potatoes and fried rabbit but died in darkness before reaching the far corners in the kitchen.

"As much supper as you got laid out, Tillie, it looks to me like y'all was expecting the preacher." He shucked off his coat and hung it and his hat from nails beside the back door and stepped to the washstand next to the stove.

"Let me dip you some hot water, Luke," she said.

"I know where the reservoir is, Tillie," he said. "You take your seat and don't bother with me."

She slipped onto her chair at Matt's left and lightly laid her fingertips on the back of his wrist. They smile at each other.

Luke washed his hands, feeling at ease in their house and their company, but the question of whether he should tell them how things stood between his pa and him rasped to and fro in his head. He stepped back to the warmth of the stove and dried his hands on a flour sack towel.

"Supper ain't really that much, Luke," Tillie said. "Matt caught a couple o' young rabbits in his traps, and you know how I love fried rabbit."

"C'mon here and set down, old son," Matt said, nodding at the chair on his right. "These cathead biscuits and taters will warm you up, inside and out."

"That's a sure enough certainty," Luke said.

"Would you say grace?" Matt's offer to let Luke say the blessing was a form of courtesy. He didn't expect Luke to accept.

"You go ahead, Matt," he said and bowed his head.

Matt tented his hands over his plate, and the blessing rolled from his mouth like wagon wheels in worn and familiar ruts.

"Amen," he said, and taking a biscuit, he passed the platter to Luke. "Dig in, old son."

"So, a couple o' rabbits stumbled in your traps, did they, Matt?" he said and grinned across the lamplight at Tillie.

"Don't set in on him about his trapping, Luke," she said.

"Yeah," Matt said. Cracking open a biscuit, he smeared it with butter. "I caught them rabbits for Tillie."

Luke noticed how much Matt favored his ma when he smiled like that.

"And I caught a coon and three minks for me. I'd druther have a good baked coon for supper myself, but he was older than Methuselah and would've been tougher than a boiled saddle. You could've smelt that coon for a quarter mile."

"How many traps you got set?" Luke bit into a rabbit leg.

"I ain't got but a dozen out, yet, but I figure on setting another two dozen. There's plenny of mink and coon sign over where Deer Branch runs into the Hennessey, but I can't seem to trap them. After supper, we'll put old Soldier and Queenie on them coons and catch 'em up a tree."

"Mighty fine rabbit, Tillie," Luke said.

"She's the best cook I've got," Matt said, and taking a bite of biscuit, he winked at Tillie.

"He means I'm the onliest cook on the place." She playfully tapped his hand.

"Any way you say it, these're mighty fine vittles," Luke said.

"As good a cook as Retty is, I suspect you're used to good eating," Tillie said. "How are the folks doing, Luke?"

Luke looked at her across the table, going over in his mind what she asked, thinking how to answer. He dropped his eyes to the small dent at the base of her throat, and lower, then to the red and white flowers in the table oilcloth.

"They was… When I left, they was just fine," he said. He looked at Matt, then at Tillie and back at Matt.

"What's the matter, Luke?" Matt said. "When I seen you in the lane, I just naturally figured you was aiming to go hunting." Matt rested his fisted hands on either side of his plate, his right gripping his fork like a hammer handle.

"Truth is, me and Pa had a falling out." He spoke, straight-out and plain, without intent of saying it or of not saying it. "I was headed for the cutoff trail, going to Seth's place when the hounds set up a row and you came out on the porch."

"Your pa's a good man, Luke. A good Christian man. But I know he can be mighty stubborn sometimes, too," Matt said. "What happened?"

"I tried to reason with him again about letting me go on my own. I'll be nineteen at the end of October, but he said he needs me to help him raise another ten acres of cotton this year for some reason. Anyhow, I said things and he said things, and I lit out headed for Seth's, but I know Seth doesn't have any work for me, and most likely, he'll take Pa's part anyhow and try to talk me into going back home. So, I figured on maybe going over to Salem and see if I could hire out there."

Nodding his head, Matt listened and occasionally glanced at Tillie. When Luke stopped talking, Matt laid his fork on his empty plate, and propping his elbows on the table, he tented his hands like he was going to say grace again. He leaned toward Luke.

"I'll tell you what, Luke. We can't pay you in money, but if you want to, if you'll help me mend the fences and chop firewood and get the cotton and corn patch ready to plant and just help out in general around the place, we'll give you a place to sleep and plenny to eat."

Luke hesitated, caught unawares. He'd expected Matt to be cajoling but not to take his side or to offer him work and a place to live.

"In the meanwhile," Matt said, "something might turn up. I unnerstand a couple of folks over at Salem, figure on planting another twenty or thirty acres in cotton this spring. If they do, they're gonna be hiring day-help come springtime."

"And I can always use help toting water and feeding the chickens," Tillie said.

"I wouldn't wanna be under foot or put y'all out none," he said. "I mean, I didn't intend…"

"You'd be a big help to me, Luke," Matt said. "Only I can't pay you no money."

"And we got plenny room in this house," Tillie said. "It ain't no trouble."

He glanced at Tillie, her eyes shining. His ma was right. Matt was lucky to make a catch like her.

"Well, how does that suit you, old son?" Matt said.

Luke felt uneasy. He knew he ought to say no and go to Seth's place and take his chances with his brother or maybe at Salem, if need be. It augured in his marrow, but here he had a certainty, and the idea of being free, of being his own man, made him determined.

"It suits me like my Sunday duds, Matt. Right down to the ground," he said and smiled.

"Good. That's settled," Matt said. He leaned back from the table and patted his stomach with both hands. "Now, get your coat on, old son, and I'll fetch my twenty-two and carbide lamp. The coons'll be prowling on a cold, dark night like tonight."

"Do y'all want some coffee before you go, Matt?" Tillie said. She rose and began clearing the dishes from the table.

"I don't think we got time, Tillie," Matt said. "We oughta be on the creek bank right now."

They pushed away from the table, chairs scraping and bumping the floor. Matt went into their bedroom to fetch his twenty-two rifle and hunting coat with the carbide headlamp and cap in the pocket. Setting her dishpan on the kitchen shelf, Tillie glanced at Luke as he stood at the back door and slipped into his coat.

"Seems mighty chilly for y'all to be traipsing around in the woods tonight," she said. She smiled at him and reached the dipper from a nail on the side of the pantry, then raised the lid of the stove reservoir.

"If it turns too cold, we'll build a fire or come on back to the house," Matt said walking into the kitchen. "Either way, we'll be back sometimes before daylight." He handed the rifle and headlamp cap to Luke. "Hold these, old son, while I pull my coat on. You leave your hat here. We'll take turns wearing the headlamp and my hat."

She dipped hot water from the stove reservoir and poured it over a square of soap in the dishpan, and they went out the door.

"Y'all be particular," she said and hung the dipper from its nail.

As they crossed the porch, Matt whistled and called, "Here Queenie! Here Soldier!" and she heard the dogs' heads bump against the floor joists as they scrambled from under the house.

"You load the lamp with carbide," Matt said, "and I'll draw a bucket of water to fill my bottle."

She lowered the supper plates into the dishwater and heard the well pulley squeak as Matt drew water for the carbide lamp.

"Here," Matt said. "I want you to wear the headlamp and shoot first so as your old uncle can learn you something about..." His words faded.

She wiped her dishrag over a plate and set it on the drain board.

"My hind foot!" Luke's voice. The back gate rattled open and banged shut.

Their dwindling voices drowned in the darkness, and she reached into the dishpan for another plate. Her hands paused, wrist deep in the hot, soapy water, and for a long moment, she stood in the silence.

Chapter Six

They came back before first light, laughing and talking. In the kitchen, the firebox door of the stove clanged open and shut as Matt rebuilt the fire to make coffee. Pots rattled and scraped.

She turned on her back and pushed her feet deeper and deeper into the cold sheets, cold as well water and opened her eyes and looked into the gray light that pushed through the bedroom window. She smiled and pulled the warm quilts over her face, drowsing in the half-sleep, half-memory of an early summer morning after daylight but before sunrise, and she and Alice, her older sister, whispered in their house-in-the-bed under counterpane roof, and full-throated blue jays yapped, and a redbird whistled and chucked outside their open window, and the bed groaned in the next room, Alice telling, her little girl's voice low and husky, where babies really came from and how a man and woman made babies together, between the woman's legs, in her stomach. Tillie didn't believe her, not Mama and Papa, but the shock and the exhilaration and the breathlessness of hearing it said, throaty words whispered in secret, made it true before she actually conceived it. She knew the groans were Mama's, too, groans deep in hidden pleasure, and she stretched full length under the counterpane, her nightgown pulled tight around her thighs. Her head swam with keening and images. Keening heard only in her ears, images of naked. Her skin prickled, and with a sudden gasp, she woke to their distant voices and the aroma of hot coffee seeping into the still room. Her heart pounded, and she lay for a moment in her warmth, savoring the slowing of her heartbeat and the laxation of muscles in her thighs and loins. Matt seldom touched her in that way after their first time. She had cried out, and there was blood. Since then, he'd acted as though he was ashamed of what they'd done, what he'd done, and didn't really want her anymore, not in that way.

The rattle and chink of china and the muted bumps of cups and saucers drew her thoughts to breakfast and Matt and Luke in the kitchen. She braced herself against the cold and threw back the quilts and sat up on the side of the bed and pulled on her socks and shoes. Standing, she slipped on her housedress over her nightgown and buttoned it, mismatching buttons to buttonholes. Feeling her way through the half-light to the dresser, she found her shawl hanging beside the mirror and draped it over her head. She tied it with a single knot under her chin and bustled from the bedroom across the dogtrot hall into the kitchen, her arms hugging her bosom.

Matt sat at the head of the table, Luke on his right. Their coffee cups steamed in front of them. Both rose from their chairs when she came into the room.

"Morning, Tillie," Matt said. "Let me pour you a cup of coffee."

"No," she said. "Both of y'all just sit down. I wanna wash my face and warm up first, and then I'll pour my coffee. Did y'all kill anything?"

"Oh, yeah," Matt said, and as he talked, she clutched the shawl at her throat with one hand, and with the other, she drew the dipper from the water pail and turned to face him and drank.

"But the end of the tale," Matt said, "is we got five nice, fat coons, thanks to my good shooting eye." He grinned at Luke.

"Good shooting eye, my hind foot," Luke said. "Matt didn't make a killing shot all night. Soldier and Queenie had to fight every coon he shot out."

She smiled and raised the lid of the stove reservoir and began dipping water into the washbasin.

"I was just teasing the hounds," Matt said. "Giving 'em a little sport."

She slipped the shawl down on her shoulders and dipping her hands into the basin of water, she washed her face.

"I'll bet old Soldier don't figure it was much sport," Luke said. "That right ear looked purty tattered to me."

She turned her back to the warmth of the stove and toweled her face.

"Ah," Matt said. "That ear bleeds if he sneezes too hard."

Again, she draped the shawl over her hair and clutched it at her throat with one hand. She said, "Y'all ready for more coffee?" She opened the china safe and set another saucer and cup for herself.

"I guess not, Tillie," Matt said. He drank the last of his coffee and clacked his cup on the saucer. "It's breaking daylight, and we gotta skin them coons."

They scraped back their chairs and rose. At the door, they lifted their coats from the nails and began pulling them on. She poured her cup full, and then set the coffeepot back on the stove.

"I'll have breakfast ready by the time y'all finish dressing the coons," she said, settling into her chair at the table.

They stepped out into the cold breaking daylight, and the door latch rattled and clicked as Matt pulled the door shut behind him. She raised the cup to her lips, blew steam from the hot surface and sipped.

*

In the backyard, Matt opened his Barlow pocketknife and fished a small whetstone from his pants pocket. He clenched the stone in his left hand between his middle finger and the heel of his thumb and slowly drew the knife blade against the grain of the rock. Luke pulled a coon from a burlap sack that lay on the edge of the porch; the soft gray and black fur was cold to the touch, and the coon's forepaws were curled under its chin. He held the coon by a foreleg and a hindleg and pulled stretching and limbering its taut muscles and joints to make the skinning easier. Matt tried the keenness of the knife blade on the ball of his thumb, grunted his satisfaction, and laid the stone on the porch.

"You hold 'em, old son, and I'll jerk the hides off 'em," Matt said. His voice smoked in the chill. "We'll be back in a warm kitchen eatin' bacon and biscuits before the cock crows."

"I can handle a bushel of that," Luke said, and stepped toward Matt, offering the coon, belly up.

"Get away from here, dogs!" Matt said. The hounds took a last sniff of the coon and backed off, and looking up at him, their sad eyes humble and submissive, they wagged their tails.

"Y'all'll get y'all's share directly," he said.

Luke stood straddle-legged to brace against the pull and tug of the skinning chore. He held the limbered coon by its hind legs, belly up and admired Matt's skill as he slit the hide with the point of his knife from the ankle of one hind leg across the crotch behind the testicles and down the other hind leg to the ankle without nicking the flesh.

"This un must've been the boar-coon of the Hennessey," Luke said.

"Appears to be," Matt said and laughed.

They gripped and pulled, peeling the skin from the carcass.

"A feller could make a purty good sized coat with that hide," Luke said.

"Or a small blanket," Matt said. He draped the skin from a peach tree branch above the hounds' reach, and grasping the coon's genitals, he cut them from the carcass. "You need a toothpick, old son? Mister Coon ain't gonna need it anymore." Grinning, he tossed the mass in the direction of the hounds, and Soldier leapt and snapped it in mid-air.

"If I need a toothpick, I'll whittle me one from a black gum twig."

The knife blade made a faint ripping sound as Matt slit open the coon's brisket and belly. He stripped out the entrails, and with a quick slice of the blade, he divided them in two and tossed a share to each hound, then hung the carcass next to the hide. Luke pulled another coon from the burlap sack and began stretching its legs as Matt pulled his knife blade over the whetstone again.

"You gonna have to hold 'em steady, old son," he said. "I can't shuck 'em and hold 'em, too."

"I got the coon. You just make certain you don't cut me with that razor."

"I don't cut what I don't aim to cut," Matt said. "And you was right about them coons stirring tonight."

"I figured they was when I saw that one cross the Buskin Road behind me on my way over here."

"I unnerstand that," Matt said and grinned. "But what I wanna know, old son, is how come you to see a coon that crossed the road behind you?"

"I turned around to see him," Luke said. "I heard a breeze rattle them dry cornstalks then I heard a crackling in the leaves on the road bank that I didn't figure was from a breeze, and naturally, I turned around to see what it was."

"Naturally," Matt said.

*

Grandma Knox said that when she was a child old folks told of a man named Abner Buskin and his wife, Molly, who built a cabin between what is now the fork of the Buskin and Salem Roads and the Buskin Bridge over Hennessey Creek. They were young folks, and Abner deadened a few acres to farm and trapped mink and coon for fur to trade for cash money to buy staple goods. His wife had their first child their second winter in that cabin with nobody but her husband for midwife. Come spring and the baby was two or three months old, and it came time for Abner to saddle up and ride to

Clemson to trade his trap hides and buy flour, sugar, salt, coffee and such as that, and he left Molly alone with the baby. When Abner got back home late the next day, the cabin was closed and quiet. No smoke rose from the chimney and no sign of life anywhere. His horse shied, they said, skittish like, and walled his eyes, so Abner jumped down and tied him to a dogwood sapling and helloed real loud, then listened. He heard a faint whining, but couldn't course it, so he commenced to look around, close and keen and saw the cabin door was scratched and clawed. He ran to the door and pulled the latchstring. In the cabin, the baby lay in its crib, whining and cooing, but no sign of his wife. Looking about, he noticed the water bucket missing, and he got vexed at her for leaving the baby alone so long to go to the creek and fetch water. He picked up the baby and started down the path that led to the creek where they drew their water. He stopped and helloed and listened. Still, no answer. He got scared then, afraid she might've slipped and fallen into the creek and drowned, and he took out running. Halfway between the cabin and the creek, he came upon Molly's body all bloody and torn.

Grandma would stop talking, taking more time than was needed to catch her breath. As the silence grew, she'd commence talking again.

Abner Buskin found panther tracks round his wife big as horse tracks. She still clutched the rope bail of the wooden bucket in her hand, and bucket staves were scattered round where she lay, so she must've swung that bucket, fighting the big cat to her dying breath. The old folks all said the panther had most likely been watching the cabin ever since Abner left and had seen her go out to fetch water, then tried to get to the baby. When she heard the big cat squalling and clawing on the door, she ran back a-hollering, and the cat turned and jumped her. They said it must've been an old panther because the only part of her that he ate was her tender, suckling breasts.

*

Luke's nose began to run.

"Hold him steady," Matt said. "Is this the last one?"

"Yeah, he's the last, but I gotta wipe my nose, Matt," Luke said. Tightening his hold on the coon's hind legs, he raised his coat sleeve to his nose.

"That's a mighty handy snotrag you got there."

"My hands are bloody. I can't reach in my pocket."

"Wipe your nose on Soldier's ear," Matt chuckled.

"He'd just wipe his nose on my ear if I did."

The smell of fried bacon drifted from the kitchen, and Luke thinking her bosom was bigger than Leah Tupper's. He'd never seen Tillie's or Leah's, but he did touch Leah's. Leah Tupper lingered in his thoughts as he braced in his stance again, and Matt peeled the skin from the coon and draped it from the peach tree limb. Three years ago, he and Seth had camped for a week and shot ducks on Nashobee Lake. She had brown eyes. They did hunt. Old Man Tupper liked them. Said they were kinfolks. Killed ducks until they ran out of shotgun shells. The smell of blood and warm down in the chilled air. Her hair black as night. Kissing kin. Warm. Would've stayed longer, but they ran out of shotgun shells. Seth married the next spring. Not a Nashobee Lake girl and Seth was his own man now, making his way, on his own.

"Hold him steady, old son," Matt said.

"Durn. I've got him, Matt. Gut him," Luke said.

"You sure this is the last un, old son?" Matt said and slit open the belly.

"Yeah, we've reached the turn-row," Luke said. "You think it's gonna freeze before the sun gets up?"

"I figure there's skim-ice in the water trough already." With a quick slice of his knife, he divided the entrails between the hounds.

"That's it, old son, and I smell the bacon a-frying. Let's go get washed up and eat some of them biscuits and bacon."

"What d'you wanna do with the carcasses and the hides?"

"Leave 'em hanging where they are. The hounds can't reach 'em, and we'll take this young one in for the cook." Matt climbed the porch steps and stopped at the kitchen door and nodded at the peach tree. "After breakfast, if you'll milk old Belle, I'll hang the carcasses in the smokehouse and stretch the hides, and later while we pull and burn last year's cornstalks, I'll learn you how to tell the difference between a coon's eye and a star."

They walked into the warmth of the kitchen and the smell of fried bacon and hot biscuits.

"You was the one that said to shoot, durn you."

"I meant for you to shoot the coon's eye, old son, not a blamed star."

"There wa'n't no coon's eye. It was a star shining through a clump of moss."

"That's what I say. I'm gonna learn you the difference."

Tillie hummed as she set the table. Dressed in her day clothes, she no longer wore the shawl over her head, and her hair hung down her back in a single, loose plait.

"Y'all're just in time for breakfast," she said.

"We'd been in sooner," Luke said. "But you know how Matt dawdles when it comes to cleaning coons." He dipped hot water from the reservoir into the washbasin and scrubbed the clotted blood from his hands and around his fingernails.

"Baked coon for supper, Tillie," Matt said. "Thanks to my good shootin' eye." He laid the dressed coon in a clean dishpan on the shelf and reached his hands into the wash basin with Luke. Luke jostled him with his hip.

"Good shootin' eye, my hind foot," Luke said. He unhooked the flour sack towel from its nail and backed to the hot stove. Drying his hands on the towel, he smiled at Tillie when she looked up from the table.

"I done forgot more than I learnt you about huntin' and fishin' and trappin', old son," Matt said. "And if you'd shot one more star this morning, you would've ruptured my little old twenty-two rifle with the strain." He snatched the towel from Luke's hands.

"Either way, y'all are gonna have to fetch me in a coupla armloads of stove wood if I'm gonna bake a coon and sweet potatoes."

"First thing after breakfast, Tillie," Matt said as they settled around the table. "Then Luke's gonna milk old Belle while I stretch them coon hides, and then we're gonna start pulling last year's cornstalks. Soon as we catch up on the work, I'm gonna set more traps in the next couple weeks or so, and we'll get started with the plowing quick as it's dry enough," he said and chuckled.

"What's tickled you, Matt?" she asked.

"Luke says them dead cornstalks make a terrible racket in the night breeze."

"Grandma Knox's ghost stories ain't got you spooked, have they Luke?" she said and smiled.

"Grandma Knox's ghosts ain't no bother to me, Tillie," Luke said. "They ain't real and if they was, they can't do nothing more than scare a feller. But I do put a lot of stock in her panther tales. It ain't been but a couple o' years ago that we was trailed through the swamp by a panther, and he's real, and he can maul a feller mighty bad."

"That's a sure enough certainty," Matt said, and nodding his head, he took a biscuit and passed the platter to Luke. "Here, grab you a couple o' these cat head biscuits, old son, and I'll say grace."

Chapter Seven

A fire burned in the fireplace in the big front room which served as parlor, sewing room, and Retty and Thurston's bedroom.

"Ma, can I go outside?" Asa asked.

"I wanna go, too," Callie said.

"Alright, but just for a little while."

Asa broke for the door.

"Y'all put on your coats," Retty said. "And stay on the sunny side of the house. It's still chilly."

"Yessum," Asa said, and he and Callie pulled on their coats as they went out the door.

"I suppose we can get some stitching done on the new quilt today, girls," Retty said. "With your pa gone, I don't figure on fixing much for dinner today, and we can get a lot done before we have to start fixing supper. Sarah, you fetch our sewing baskets, honey, while me and Maud lower the quilting frame."

The six by eight-foot quilting frame hung over Retty and Thurston's bed suspended from the ceiling by four cords, one fastened to each corner of the frame. The cords ran over four hooks screwed into the ceiling. When they were not sewing on the quilt, the frame was pulled to the ceiling by the cords, and the cords tied to nails in the wall.

"Ma, how long are you gonna keep me from talking to Joe?" Maud asked as they lowered the quilting frame. "You know he expects to come to see me Saturday evening."

Sarah brought their sewing baskets and set them on the edge of the quilting frame.

"You're just gonna have to let me think on it awhile, Maud," she said. "You girls pull chairs over here for yourselves and the rocking chair for me."

Scraping and bumping the floor, they set the chairs at the sides of the frame, and taking their places around the quilt, they rummaged in their sewing baskets for needles and thread.

"Did I put my specs in one of y'all's baskets?" Retty said. "No, never mind. I found 'em." She took the spectacles from among the thread spools, needles, scissors, and cloth scraps in her basket, unfolded the legs and hooked them behind her ears. "I declare, I think I would lose my head this morning if it wa'n't setting on my shoulders."

Retty broke a short length of thread, put one end in her mouth to wet it and twisted it to a finer point. Holding the needle and thread up to the light, she pushed the thread through the eye of the needle.

"I think Pa would unnerstand that it was just a dirty-mouthed little boy's slur," Maud said.

Retty was worried about Thurston. He had been acting out of sorts lately, and with Luke running off the way he did, she was afraid he was even more aggravated. He hardly spoke at breakfast and seemed in more of a hurry than usual when he saddled Button and rode out before daylight going to his pa's place to help mark shoats.

"Maybe, so, Maud," Retty said and slipped her thimble onto the tip of her middle finger. "I'll talk to him tonight. Hopefully, it ain't no more 'n what you say it is." Carefully, she pushed her needle through the quilt.

And she knew that she had loved Thurston Knox from the moment he kissed her.

*

Her pa, Rufus Tarroll, had been a farmer, but he also ran a cotton gin, gristmill, and a blacksmith shop, and in appreciation of his patrons and to try to obligate others, he would throw a big play-party after picking-time. Everybody he could reach from Salem to Clemson was invited to his place usually on the last Saturday in October. On the Friday before she first saw Thurston, she and her ma and her younger sister, Hannah, baked bread and cakes and swept and scrubbed the house and brush-broomed the yards clean. Her pa and her older brother, Doss, butchered two steers and several pigs. Near the blacksmith shop, they spitted the beeves and pigs on peeled hickory poles and set the ends of the poles on iron posts her pa had made on his forge and anvil. Well into the night, they fed a side-fire with seasoned hickory blocks and from it, shoveled glowing coals under the meat and sipped whiskey.

"Just to keep our heads clear for the chore," her pa said, and winked.

Occasionally, her pa or Doss walked to the spits and with a butcher knife, sliced morsels of beef or pork and passed it around. A little while before midnight, her ma led her and Hannah into the house, and she went to bed so excited about the coming party that she felt she would never sleep again. In bed, she watched the flickers of light from the outside cook-fire lick her bedroom walls and ceiling, and somewhere between sleep and waking, she drifted into the play-party frolic with her best friend, Mavis MacFarland, as they danced, talked and played party games. Then, she woke, and it was daylight on the day she first saw Thurston Knox.

She was seventeen and most folks, including her, took it as a settled matter that she and Lum Kendall would be married, though no such words had ever passed between them. Lum was twenty years old, lean, with brown hair and a reddish mustache and blue eyes that crinkled in the corners when he smiled. Every year after Lum and his pa picked and ginned their cotton, Retty's pa hired him as extra help at the gin and gristmill. He worked hard, saved his money and spoke openly to Retty about saving enough money to buy the eighty acres that adjoined the Tarroll farm on one side and his pa's place on the other. His saving with intent to buy the acreage was often the subject of his talk when he came to sit with her in the parlor or on the front porch swing, but he never mentioned marriage to her and had only kissed her by the rules of play-party games. Retty accepted this as usual courtship until Mavis, who had not yet married Retty's brother, Doss, had not yet thought of Doss in that way, told her differently. Mavis had older, married sisters, and they knew such things.

"Retty," Mavis had said her gray eyes wide with amazement. "Don't you know a feller kisses his girl at every chance and even, sometimes, touches her like she wants but oughtn't to allow." Then she smiled and turned her head as though she'd run out of patience with a stubborn child.

Around noontime the day of the play-party, guests began to drive up in wagons and carts and to ride in on horseback. They came from as far as Clemson to the southeast and Salem to the northwest, and they all ate. Then the older folks, men and women, stood around the yards or sat on the porches and talked crops, hounds, cough remedies, cake recipes, or politics while the unmarried young folks courted and flirted in sight of but out of earshot of the grown-ups and the children played out-of-doors games. As darkness crept out of the woods into the yards, some folks bade goodbye, and others arrived and ate, joined by some taking seconds and then, all moved into the house, and the dancing began.

Retty sashayed round the square with Lum and tilted back her head to blow a strand of hair from her face and saw Thurston come into the room with Horace Odom, but she didn't know his name, yet. A smile drew his black mustache at the corners of his mouth as he looked round the room and pulled his hat brim across his dark eyes. He stuck one fist on his hip and propped his other hand high against the doorjamb and watched as the dancers stepped and swung round the floor. Something in his stance and appearance and the exhilaration of the dance caught Retty up on impulse. She promenaded round Lum, put her palm next to her mouth, and shouted over the music, "Take off your hat, mister, and stay a little while!"

He pushed himself upright from the doorjamb and grinned at her, his teeth all white under his black mustache. A blush flamed Retty's hairline and spread down her face and throat. Horace Odom guffawed loudly and slapped Thurston's back. She felt foolish and confused and dropped a step and had to skip to pick it up. She glanced at Lum and looked round the room, but Lum watched their feet, trying to catch her misstep, and no one seemed to have heard her but Thurston and Horace.

What's the matter with you, Retty? She thought. *You don't know that fellow from Job's turkey.* As she danced past him the second time, she tried not to look in his direction, but he doffed his hat and made a sweeping bow.

Thank goodness, the set ended before she passed him again, and Lum escorted her to her chair beside Mavis in front of an open window. An early frost had fallen the week before, but a warm spell had set in, and the smoky parlor, lighted with coal oil lamps, was stuffy and buzzed with chatter and laughter. Adding to the din and excitement, the guitar player and fiddler strummed and sawed their way into the next set. Retty waved a palmetto fan under her flushed face and looked toward the door, but the young man who'd bowed to her was gone.

"Alright, you young bucks!" Charley Lufkin, the fiddler, shouted over the din. "And you ole bucks, too, if ya still got it in ya, it's time for a buck an' wing. You young ladies look 'em over 'cause y'all're gonna get to pick ya one for the next set!" And he pulled the bow across the strings of his fiddle and broke into *Ida Red.* Among the other men, Horace Odom and Thurston pushed the balls of their feet across the floor dropping their heels on the downbeat.

"Who's that feller that came in with Horace Odom?" Retty asked Mavis behind her fan.

Mavis raised her fan to her lips and said, "That's Thurston Knox."

"Do you know him?"

"Why, yes," Mavis said. "He's George and Onie Knox's oldest boy from over on the other side of Hennessey Creek. I figured y'all was acquainted by the way you spoke to him."

Bareheaded now, Thurston danced, elbows lifted in flight.

"I've heard folks speak of the Knoxs," she said. "How come I've never seen him before?"

"Oh, you've seen him before. I 'spect his pa gins here every year like most folks within ten miles. Besides," she said and lowered her voice, "folks say his ma, Miz Onie Knox is part some kinda Indian or something."

"Be that as it may, Mavis, I don't sit around and watch ever'body that comes here to gin cotton or grind cornmeal," Retty said. "I ain't ever seen him before." She tried to fix her eyes on Lum or Doss, but as the buck and wing came to an end, she found herself watching Thurston.

"Alright, ladies!" Charley Lufkin shouted as the dancers cleared the floor. "Now y'all seen 'em, pick ya one and dance him through the floor!"

"This is your chance to get to know Mr. Thurston Knox," Mavis said and smiled at her. "Ask him to dance."

"I will not!" she said. And she rose, laid her fan on her chair seat, and walked across the room and made her curtsy to Lum. As he escorted her onto the floor, she watched Mavis to see if she would ask Thurston to dance. She chose Retty's pa.

Retty's pa was a tall, rotund man, well into his fifties. He worked hard but loved fun and frolic, and everybody called him Rufe or Mr. Rufe. Retty noticed that throughout the set, Mavis kept up a constant chatter, and her pa nodded and grinned. She giggled to herself, doubting he understood a word Mavis said through his creeping deafness and the loud music. Later Retty knew that her pa had understood at least some of what Mavis had said because when the set ended, he stepped into the middle of the floor and waved his arms.

"Alright, folks! We're gonna have a game of hog-hunters. Lum, you and Doss bring a coupla them chairs out here."

"Pa's commencing the games early tonight," Retty said.

"I told him I figured he oughta," Mavis said, "seeings how they're folks here from the other side of Hennessey Creek that are practically strangers. Give us a chance to make their acquaintance." She smiled and turned her head.

As Lum and Doss fetched the chairs and stood them side by side, facing opposite directions, the ladies bustled back to their chairs to collect their fans.

"C'mon and set by me, Retty," her pa called. He sat in one chair and patted the seat of the other, and she threaded her way through the crowd. "We gotta spell these folks with a game of hog-hunters before they burn out a-dancing."

She took her place next to him to play the part of the oldest "daughter," her back straight, her chin up and waved her fan at her bosom. She searched the faces of the young bachelors as they pranced, circling her and her pa, not quite sure why until she saw Thurston and looked into his eyes. With his fists on his hips, he strutted with the other young men, and she felt what Mavis's sisters said must be true. She didn't think in her head, *I want him to kiss me and touch me like I oughtn't allow*, but she felt it in the pit of her stomach, and her heart began to race to the rhythm of the prancing feet. She lowered her eyes, color rising in her hairline.

"Mavis!" Mr. Rufe said. "You and Lum c'mon in the circle, and Charley," he called to the fiddler. "Raise the roof, lad!"

Charlie tapped his foot on the floor, cradled his fiddle and bent his ear over the strings. Then, drawing his bow, he jumped into the tune.

Mavis and Lum joined hands and promenaded around Retty and her pa inside the circle of young bachelors and sang, almost chanted,

"Now this is my daughter that sets by my side,

"And no hog-hunter can get her for his bride,

"And you can't get lodging here,

"Oh, you can't get lodging here!"

The bachelor hog-hunters circled and strutted and sang in answer,

"Your daughter is pretty, you're ugly yourself,

"So, we'll travel on further and seek better wealth,

"And we don't want lodging here,

"No, we don't want lodging here!"

Her pa sat straight in his chair and floated his hand in front of himself keeping time with the music and cleared his throat. He always did this to build up the suspense about which partner he'd choose for his "daughter," but Retty knew, as most everyone in the room knew, that he'd surely choose Lum for her again.

He sang loudly,

"Now this is my daughter that sets by my side,

"And Thurston Knox can have her for his bride,

"And he can get lodging here,

"Oh, he can get lodging here!"

Her heart leapt, Retty later told Mavis, like John the Baptist in Elisabeth's womb! Her pa always called Lum's name. The buzz in the room almost hushed then laughter and chatter rose again. Retty blushed, and glanced at Lum, but he hadn't noticed. Laughing, he talked into Mavis's ear.

*

Retty hadn't seen Mavis in two years, though they wrote to each other fairly often. They had been close neighbors until Doss got "Texas fever," and nothing would do him until he sold out to Matt, and they left for Texas.

"You will talk to Pa about Joseph tonight, won't you Ma?" Maud said.

Retty blinked her eyes and looked across the quilt at her.

"I'll either talk to your pa or decide for myself, Maud," Retty said. "Now go fetch them young'uns into this house. I plumb forgot about them being outside."

Chapter Eight

Seth reined his mule to a halt at the side gate and sat loosely astride the docile beast. He dreaded what he had to tell his pa. Three hounds ran along the inside of the picket fence, barking.

"Hush," he said. "You damn biscuit eaters."

The dogs recognized Seth and anxiously wagged their tails and whined.

He swung his right leg up and over the mule's neck, slid to the ground and looped the cotton rope reins over a picket. As he straightened the burlap sack on the mule's back that he used for a riding pad, he looked about. Nothing but the dogs seemed to stir on the place until a hen cackled from the far side of the house, and a rooster flapped his wings and strutted across the yard between the kitchen-house and barn lot, the sun shone hard and bright on his yellow feathers. Stopping, he stretched himself on his toes, and crowed.

"Yeah, big mouth," Seth muttered. "Ever'body knows she laid your egg." He bent his head over his opened palm and dropped a spent cud of chewing tobacco from his mouth into his hand and tossed it into the Buskin Road.

Asa and Callie crawled from under the back porch and brushed dust from their hands and knees. They saw Seth and waited, sheepishly surprised, until he looked at them.

"You young'uns better not let Pa catch y'all playing under that house," he said. He lifted the gate latch and stepped in the yard. The hounds ran to him.

"Get down, dogs!" he scolded.

Their pa had told Luke and him not to dig holes under the house. "It'll weaken the foundation ground," he'd said. "The house blocks will sink and cause the floor to sag."

"Pa's gone over to Grandma and Grandpa's," Asa said.

"Luke ran away from home, yesterday," Callie said.

"I know what Luke done," Seth said. "How come Pa's gone to Grandpa's?" And he thought, *Gone to Grandpa's. At least I won't be facing Pa with the news.*

"They gonna mark pigs," Asa said.

"Where's Ma?" Seth said. *I don't see how come Pa didn't just free Luke in the first place. Nineteen come this fall. Go when he pleases. Can't see why Pa's being so contrary about it.*

"In the big front room," Asa said. "They're sewing a quilt." He picked his nose and rubbed his slick fingertip on his britches leg.

"Y'all stay out from under the house," Seth said and started up the back porch steps.

"Tattletale," Asa said.

"I don't tattle on nobody, son," Seth said, pausing on the top step. "But if I catch y'all under that house again, I'll tan y'all's hide myself."

"Tattletale, tattletale!" Asa said.

"Hanging on a bull's tail!" Callie said. She put her fists on her waist and swung her hips from side to side.

Seth made a move as though to go back down the steps, and Asa and Callie giggled, and grabbing at each other, they scrambled for the corner of the house, looking over their shoulders, eyes wild with gleeful fright.

Seth smiled and shook his head as the back door opened, and Maud stepped out onto the porch, pulling on her sweater. Her brown eyes crinkled in a smile when she saw him.

"Why, howdy, Seth," she said. "I didn't hear you come up. How's Martha and Nathan?"

"Just fine. Ever'body here well?"

"As well as can be expected after what Luke's gone and pulled. Did he come home with you?" She looked beyond him at the mule tethered to the picket fence.

"No," he said. "I can't say as I blame him neither. Y'all quilting?"

"Yeah, but Ma sent me to call the young'uns in outta the cold. Did you see 'em?"

"They just ran around the house. How's Joe Burgess these days?"

"How would I know?"

Seth smiled. Something was amiss.

"I suppose I just figured you're a good guesser, I guess." He grinned.

"I am," she said and hugging her sweater closed across her bosom, she skipped down the steps and started round the house.

Seth shrugged his shoulders, opened the door, and stepped into the big room. His ma and Sarah sat at the quilting frame. With her arm raised in the middle of drawing a stitch, his ma peered at him over her spectacles. He doffed his hat.

"Morning, son," she said. "I don't see him, so I don't suppose Luke come home with you?" She angled her needle into the quilt, removed her spectacles and laid them inside her sewing basket.

"No, ma'am," he said. He held his hands in the heat from the fireplace then stooped and laid on another stick of firewood. "But I saw him."

"Where at?" she said and pressed her curled forefinger to her pursed lips.

"Over at Matt's place. I rode over there to borrow Matt's leather awl to sew up one of my old mule collars, and when I come up, I caught him and Luke headed to the field to pull cornstalks. It looks like Matt and Tillie took him in." He turned his back to the hearth as the flames caught hold on the freshly laid log.

"Huh. That ain't gonna set none too well with your pa."

"I don't figure it will either, but there it is," Seth said. "I talked to him, tried to tell him he oughta come on back home, but he wouldn't have none of it, and he asked me to ride over here and fetch his clothes for him."

"I guess that worked to the good, anyways. Your pa rode over to help your grandpa and your Uncle Morgan mark shoats this morning and won't be back till late. He's gonna have a fit about Matt interfering between him and Luke." She leaned forward and rose from her chair and faced Seth. "How's Martha and Nathan doing?"

"They're fine, Ma. How're you feeling?"

"I'm about fit to be tied," she said. "Luke and your pa at loggerheads about something they shouldn't be, and Maud and Joe to worry about. Will you be staying for dinner?"

"No, ma'am, I gotta head on back home," he said. "But I don't see how come Pa didn't just let Luke go in the first place. He'll be of age in a few months."

"I declare, I can't unnerstand it neither, Seth. Not for the life of me. Your pa is bound to have his reasons, but regardless, Luke oughtn't to have just run off the way he did. Take a chair, and I'll gather up a few of Luke's duds." She talked over her shoulder as she walked into the boys' bedroom and closed the door.

Rubbing his hands together, Seth crossed the room and sat in his ma's rocking chair across the quilting frame from Sarah. If she had a sweetheart, nobody knew it.

"Things got purty exciting around here the last day or two, ain't they, Sarah?"

"It's one thing atop another," she said. She glanced at Seth, then pushed her needle through the quilt and drew another stitch.

"What's this about Joe Burgess? How come Maud's got her nose outta joint with Joe Burgess?"

"Asa got in a fight with Walter, Joe's little brother, at church."

"Durn," Seth said. "They ain't taking sides in little boy squabbles, are they?"

"There's more to it than that," Sarah said. She glanced over her shoulder at the closed door.

"What more?" Seth leaned forward in his chair. Sarah liked being the first to tell the most recent news, but she made it as hard to get as picking the meat from a black walnut.

She glanced at the door again and back at him, her blue eyes and rosy face bright with gossip.

"Of course, Pa tanned Asa's britches for fightin' at church," she said. "And when we got home and Pa and Luke were out unhitching the wagon, Ma corralled Asa in the kitchen and fussed at him again about fighting and tearing his shirt and that's when he told it. Pa still don't know it." She pegged her needle into the quilt, and leaning back in her chair, she looked at Seth.

"What did Asa tell?" *She's gonna make me pick the walnut one morsel at a time.*

"He told Ma how come he was fighting with Walter Burgess." She watched him but said nothing more.

"Why was he fighting Walter?" He pried one more morsel from the cracked nut.

"Because Walter said Maud's drawers stink."

Seth grinned and nodded, knowing she would continue telling, now, until she gave out of breath or finished her story.

"Me and Maud was right there, placing cups and saucers for coffee, and Maud dropped one of Ma's blue willow cups, and I thought Ma was gonna drop her teeth."

"'How does Walter Burgess know what Maud's unnergarments smell like?' Ma said after she caught her breath.

"'I don't know, Ma. Ask Maud,' Asa said.

"'You better go on up in the house and change outta them Sunday clothes and don't say nothing to your pa about this, unless he asks you,' Ma said.

"And when he was gone, Ma asked Maud, her face pale as a hen's egg and her eyes bright as a noonday sky, 'Why would Walter Burgess say such a thing?'

"'I don't know, Ma,' Maud said. 'I guess he's just a dirty-mouthed little boy!'

"'Or maybe,' Ma said, 'he's little corn with big ears repeating what he's heard a dirty-mouth big boy say.'

"'I don't think Joe would say such as that, Ma.'

"'Well, from here on out,' Ma said, 'you just keep your distance from Mr. Joe Burgess. I'm afraid if your pa caught wind of it, it might cause an unnecessary row.'"

Seth grinned, and Sarah leaned back in her chair, proud she had told him the news first.

"Seems to me like, y'all all took sides in a little boy's squabble," Seth said.

Sarah started to answer him, but the door opened, and Retty came back into the room with a bundle of clothes. Seth stood.

"This is a coupla shirts and another pair of britches and some drawers and socks," Retty said. "But I ain't sending him his Sunday suit. He can come fetch it hisself, or when he gets rich, he can buy him some better." She handed Seth the bundle.

"Yes, ma'am," he said.

"I'll heat the morning coffee if you'll stay and drink," she said.

"No, ma'am," he said. "I need to head on back home before Martha sets in to worrying. I left home intending just to go to Matt's place, but Luke asked me to fetch him some more clothes, and I figured I oughta come let y'all know where he's at." He leaned across the bundle and kissed her forehead.

"Give Martha and Nathan our love," she said.

"I'll do that, Ma."

"And when you go out, tell Maud to bring them young'uns into this house."

*

Thurston rode in before dark and unsaddled Button in the barn. As he walked into the warmth of the kitchen-house, Retty slid a pan of biscuits into the oven and slammed the door shut.

"Sarah, you go ahead and slice some bacon, honey, and Maud, you get out a skillet to fry the bacon," she said. "Did y'all finish working the shoats, Thurston?"

"Yeah," he said. "We had plenny of unexpected help. Sid Burgess and Joe came by a little after noontime and gave us a hand."

Maud glanced at her pa but saw no change in his expression when he spoke Joe's name.

"That was mighty neighborly of them," Retty said. "The milking pail is washed and ready, and I'm gonna give you a hand with the milking and feeding." She dipped water from the stove reservoir into the rinse pail. *Chance to talk to him alone. Better now than later. Can't put Maud off any longer.* She handed Thurston the rinse pail and reached her coat from a nail by the door.

"Don't bother, Retty," he said. "You stay indoors. It's a mite chilly out."

"Maud, you and Sarah keep an eye on them biscuits and finish fixing supper," she said, slipping into her coat. "We can finish up quicker together, Thurston and get back in the house sooner."

He nodded and followed her out the door carrying the pails. From her tone of voice, he knew her purpose in helping him was more than feeding the stock and milking. Maybe she had heard something from Luke and wanted to talk to him out of earshot of the young'uns.

"I'll catch ole Penny and milk while you feed," she said and took the lead rope from the gatepost.

"Alright, I'll set the milk pails next to the milking stall."

Leaving the barn door ajar for her, he walked through the familiar stock and grain and dust smell of the barn hall. *Probably Luke*. He sat the pails in the milking stall, and taking a match from his coat pocket, he raised the lantern globe and lit the wick. He stepped across the hall to the corn crib thinking, *She's heard something from Luke for sure*. As he tore shucks from the corn, Retty led Penny into the barn and closed the door.

"Did you hear from Luke today?"

"Yeah, I did," she said and tied the lead rope at the feed trough. "Seth came by and picked up some clothes for him."

"Seth. Seth ain't took him in, has he?"

"No, but Matt did," she said, and placing the milking stool next to Penny, she sat and dipped a washrag into the rinse pail. The water warmed her cold hands.

"Matt? Matt knows he oughtn't to interfere between me and Luke," he said. He frowned and gave his head a quick shake.

"He oughta know better," she said and began to milk. "But there's another thing I wanna mention to you." The milk ripped into the bottom of the pail, and she glanced at him over her shoulder as he stepped round her.

"What's that?"

He twisted an ear of corn in his hands, and the grains pecked and bounced on the tongue-smoothed boards of the feed trough.

"About why Asa got in a fight with Walter Burgess on Sunday."

"I figured they got in a little boy's row down at the spring. Luke and those older fellers oughta keep a closer eye on them young'uns."

"Well," she said. "They got in a row because Walter said Maud's unnergarments stink."

"Ump," he grunted a short laugh and said, "I'm proud he took up for his sister, Retty, but I couldn't allow him to think it's alright to fight at church."

"Course not," she said. "But I was afraid what Walter may've heard Joe say. That Joe may've said something…"

"Retty, that's little boys bickerin' and baitin' each other," he said. "Joe Burgess is a fine young feller, and if he or Sid or Fleeta heard what Walter said, he'd get a good switching, too."

"I suppose you're right, Thurston, but you know every old crow thinks her chicks are the blackest," she said. "And I'm of half a mind to let Fleeta Burgess know just what her nasty mouthed little boy said."

"No, no, Retty," he said. "We oughta do what we can to put Asa and Walter on good terms."

"I suppose that's the Christian thing to do," she said, relieved that Thurston saw the commotion as nothing more than little boys bickering, and she felt a little ashamed that she had not taken it the same at the start.

"Yeah, and I've got an idee that Walter's brother is gonna be Asa's brother-in-law before long," he said and walked to the mules' stalls, pulling another ear of corn from his coat pocket.

PART II

Chapter Nine

February 19, 1906

"Luke, old son, if you'll milk Belle and feed the mules this morning, I thought I'd start the week setting a dozen more traps," Matt said and sipped the last of his coffee.

"Sure nuff, Matt," Luke said.

"Have y'all caught up with the field work, Matt?" Tillie asked and laid her fingertips on his wrist.

"You know we never catch up on the work, Tillie," Matt said. "But with Luke's help the last couple weeks, we got the cotton stalks and cornstalks pulled and burnt and the field fences fixed."

"Well, I suppose it's too wet to plow, yet," she said and smiled.

"Oh, yeah," he said. "But if the rain holds off a couple more days, we can start breaking the fields. You ready, old son?"

"You gather your tools and I'll gather mine," Luke said.

*

They left Tillie clearing the dishes from the table and walked to the barn in the dawn chill. Matt balanced his twenty-two rifle on his shoulder and carried a skinned rabbit for trap bait in a burlap sack. At each set, Matt would cut a slice of rabbit flesh the size of the ball of his thumb and fasten it to the trigger of the trap.

Luke, a step behind, carried a clean rag in a pail of warm rinse water in one hand and a milking pail in the other. Matt pulled open the barn door, and they entered the hay and livestock smell of the barn hall. The four stalls on the left side of the hall penned two mules, a milk cow and Matt's saddle horse, Nubbin, and the three on the right served as a milking stall, corncrib, and a storage room for harness collars, hames and plow stocks and saddle, saddle blanket and bridles and steel traps.

Matt swung open the doors to the mules' stalls and let them wander single file along the hall through the open door into the barn lot. Luke set the milking pail and rinse-water pail inside the milking stall and took a short rope from a nail on the wall.

"When you're done with the milking, old son, you might wanna pitch a couple forks of fodder from the loft for the mules and old Belle," he said and stepped into the storage room.

"I'll do it, Matt," Luke said and opened the cow stall, slipped the rope over Belle's horns and led her to the milking stall.

Matt squatted by a pile of double spring steel traps, and untangling the trap chains, he sorted through them. He figured if he caught enough coons and minks, he could make enough money selling the hides to pay Luke a few dollars for his work. Shaking his head, he mused on what Thurston might say to him about giving Luke work. It was less than a week until the third Sunday church meeting, and he would have to face his brother-in-law. Thurston was sure to be hot under the collar with him for taking Luke in, but why didn't Thurston agree to let Luke go to work for himself? Thurston could be stubborn and hot-headed, but Luke would be of an age to go when and where he pleased come October. After he weighed the fitness of a trap for his sets, he either slipped it into the burlap sack with the rabbit carcass or tossed it to the far side of the pile.

Tillie's red rooster strutted and crowed in the chicken yard, and Matt picked the last of twelve traps and bagged it.

"How's the milk coming?" he said and took the horse bridle from its nail.

"Old Belle is an easy milker," Luke said. "I might near beat the rooster's crowing this morning."

"Yeah, she's gentle and willing," Matt said and walked into Nubbin's stall, bridled him and walked him into the barn hall. "If you would, after you feed the chickens and gather the eggs, give Tillie a hand with whatever she needs, stove wood or water." He swung the saddle onto Nubbin's back.

"I'll stay handy," Luke said, walking Belle out the barn door. "You just make some good sets."

"Oh, yeah," Matt said. He stepped into the corn crib and took two ears of corn and dropped them into the sack with the traps and bait. He tied the sack to the saddle horn and holding the rifle in his left hand, led Nubbin from the barn.

*

Looking through the window over the kitchen shelf, Tillie watched Matt lead Nubbin out the back lot gate and shut and latch it then mount and ride into the woods. Alone, Luke walked toward the house with the milking pails.

Tillie stooped and reached her milk crock from under the shelf and set it on the table. Pulling open a drawer of the china safe, she found a clean cloth to cover the bowl and a length of sacking twine. Hearing Luke's footsteps on the porch, she hurried and opened the door for him, and the morning chill rushed into the warm kitchen.

"Let me have the milk, Luke," she said, and her warm hands covered his for a moment as she took the pail. "Take off your coat and warm yourself."

"Just let me warm my hands," he said. He shut the door and unbuttoned his coat as she set the milking pail on the kitchen shelf.

"It's chilly this morning, ain't it, Luke?" she said.

Edging between her and the table, his hip brushed against her, and a familiar excitement stirred in his belly. He quickly stretched his hands toward the stove and rubbed them together.

"Just a mite more than chilly," he said, and slowly turning his back to the stove, he looked at her. She glanced up from pouring the milk, smiled then lowered her eyes to her work.

"I'll heat the coffee as soon as I get the milk poured up," she said.

"If it's all the same with you, Tillie, I'll feed and gather the eggs then have coffee."

"No hurry, Luke," she said. Intent on her chore, she smiled, her brow slightly furrowed. "You go ahead, and we'll sit for our coffee when you finish." She spread the clean cloth over the crock bowl.

As he buttoned his coat, she slowly tied the cloth in place with a piece of twine. He edged between her and the table again and held his breath as his hip brushed against her.

*

Matt looked up from his last trap set and watched a man on horseback riding down the creek on the opposite bank. He recognized Horace Odom. Horace had not seen him yet.

"Howdy, Horace," Matt said and stood.

"Say there, Matt," Horace said. "I didn't see you there. Settin' for coon or mink?"

"Both."

"Having any luck?"

"Not much. Plenny of sign, and Luke and me killed a couple coons the other night, but they don't seem to take to my bait."

"What you baitin' with?"

"Fresh rabbit and I scattered a handful of corn at ever' setting."

"That oughta get coon or mink."

"Are you doin' any trapping?" Matt asked. Holding his rifle in his right hand and taking a hold on the saddle pommel with his left, he stepped up in the stirrup iron and swung astride Nubbin.

"Naw, I kinda gave up on fur trapping. I'm down here looking for a good place for a hog pen trap. I got some shoats I wanna catch up and castrate and mark before hot weather sets in."

"Well, I don't own a mark myself but I generally help Thurston work his stock and he furnishes me with plenny of pork and beef."

"I was by and saw Thurston the day before yesterday," Horace said. "He's a little bit hobbled and bruised up."

"What's his trouble?"

"Seems he was plowing new ground and hung a plow point in a root and the plow handle stove in his ribcage purty good. But he's back working. You know he's tough as a ox, Matt."

"That's a fact," Matt said and gave a short laugh.

"Say, you mentioned you and Luke coon hunting the other night," Horace said. "Ben was with me when I stopped by Thurston's place, and Asa told Ben that Luke had run away from home."

"Yeah. Thurston and Luke had a falling out," Matt said and shook his head. "You know, Luke's almost of an age to go on his own, and he's been pestering Thurston to let him go now instead of later. Thurston can be, like a feller says, bullheaded and wouldn't agree to it. Anyhow, Luke lit out and came by the house one evening a couple of weeks ago. He was talking about going to Seth's or some such, and I told him he could stay with us and give me a hand."

"You probably did the right thing, keeping him close to home for now."

"That's what I figured, too."

"By the way, is it gonna crowd your trapping, if I build a hog pen trap on this side of the creek?"

"Not a-tall, Horace. You set your pen anywhere it works best for you, and God willing, I'll see you at church on Sunday if not before."

"Sure nuff, Matt."

With a nudge of his heels, Matt started Nubbin toward home.

I ought not have interfered, Matt thought. *But Luke was determined to go somewhere, and he was apt to get hisself in trouble.*

Chapter Ten

"Are you sure it's alright for me to leave you, Tillie?" Matt said. In the dresser mirror, he watched his fingers nimbly knot his tie.

"I'm fine, Matt," she said and sat up in bed. "It's just gittin' to be my monthly headache, and it's just a slight headache. You go on to church. The deacons meet today, and your name is sure to be put up."

"I won't be in the meeting, Tillie," he said and smiled at her in the mirror.

"I know that, darling, but you should be at church. Besides, we want to know if Thurston is alright, know if he's not hurt any worse than what Horace said he was."

"I figure Horace told it the way it is," he said.

"I'm sure he knew what he was talking about," she said. "But you go on to church and make sure then you'll know what to tell Luke. I'll be fine."

"You know Luke wouldn't want to face Thurston even if he had his Sunday suit," Matt said. "He kept at me about doing some work around the place while I'm gone so I finally told him he could fix the door hinges on Nubbin's stall."

"He's right handy," she said.

"He does take up the slack," Matt said. "He's saddling Nubbin for me now." He bent and kissed her forehead.

"I'll be back as soon as church is over," he said.

"Don't hurry on my account, Matt. I'll be fine."

*

In the barn, Luke thought about being alone with her three hours or maybe more. He spread the blanket on Nubbin's back then swung the saddle over the blanket. He'd tap on her door. *I'll see about her. Hope nothing's bad wrong with her*. He'd become used to being alone with her for a couple of hours every morning while Matt ran his trapline. He wanted to see her. Her eyes.

He led Nubbin from the barn through the lot gate into the lane as Matt crossed the porch brushing lint from the brim of his hat on his wool serge coat sleeve.

"Tillie's feeling some better," he said and walked down the steps and through the gate. "I don't think she's bad sick, but if you would, see in on her ever now and again, old son, and keep a warm fire in the cookstove."

He set his hat squarely on his head and stepped up in the stirrup and forked the saddle.

"I'll see to ever'thing while you're gone," Luke said.

"I'm obliged, old son." Matt tugged his hat brim and chucked at Nubbin and rode out the lane. Luke stood outside the gate and scuffed the ground with the soles of his shoes.

He said for me to see in on her. He glanced at the house then looked out the lane. *But he just came from there. Could get more coffee before I go to the barn*. Horse and rider turned north onto the Buskin Road. get *coffee, then see in on her, maybe*. He opened the gate, climbed the porch steps and strode up the wide dogtrot hall.

In the kitchen, Tillie stood at the stove with a cup of coffee in her hand. She still wore her nightgown, ivory colored flannel with narrow, faded green stripes. The top three buttons were unbuttoned, and he saw the soft dent at the base of her throat, and below, a vein, pale blue, branched and disappeared under the edge of the flannel.

"I thought you'd gone to the barn, Luke," she said.

He raised his eyes, and she smiled.

"I—I did. I saddled Nubbin and walked him to the front gate for Matt. I thought I'd see if you were needing anything before I go back to the barn, maybe coffee or…"

"I've already poured my coffee."

"Should you be outta bed?"

"I'm fine, Luke," she said. She sipped the coffee, looking over the rim of the cup at him, her eyes dark, not quite focused.

"You look weak-eyed to me," he said and stepped toward her. "Have you got fever?"

"I don't think so," she said, and she watched her hand as she set her coffee cup on the table, thinking it could just as well be somebody else's hand. With her eyes still lowered, she stepped to him, almost touching him, her breath quick and shallow, cool in her nostrils. She licked the tip of her tongue along her lower lip and tilted her face up, throat naked. "Feel me, Luke, and see. Am I feverish?"

Slowly, he raised his hand. Hardly breathing, he cupped his palm over the warm curve of her forehead.

"Am I, Luke?" Her voice trebled, and like when Alice told her how babies were made, her stomach tightened, sunk, loosening a yearning that warmed her loins and tingled over her breasts. Tiptoeing, she slipped her arms around his neck, her mouth yielding to his urgency. She pulled away.

"Am I, Luke?" She pressed her face to his chest. "Feverish?"

The coffee-warm taste of her in his mouth, he slipped his hands down the curve of her waist and over the swell of her hips.

"Am I?"

He nodded, his throat too tight to speak. He began to lift her gown, wondering if she would stop him. Leah Tupper always stopped him.

"Luke," she whispered. "In your bed, Luke."

*

Afterwards, their wanting and needing spent, they lay under the quilt. Tillie, her cheek against his chest, reached her arm over him and closed her eyes. *God, we made a baby in me*! She sighed. *Oh, Matt! Why didn't you? Why won't you? Don't think. Not now. Oh, why*?

Luke stretched on his back, his arm under her shoulders, and stared at the ceiling. *Can't believe she let me! Damn, she's purty. Let you? Old son, she made you*!

She groaned deep in her throat and pulled closer to him. She'd seen it in his eyes, the wanting. She knew it was true at that very moment and she smiled at him, and his ears reddened, and Matt leaned over his plate, offering him room and board and didn't even notice. And when he hesitated, she said without thinking, quickly, "We got plenny of room," and Luke looked at her and said, "Yes." And Tillie knew it was true in that very moment, that somewhere, some time, there was a time and a place because he wanted her, and her need was to be wanted, and Matt didn't even notice.

Damn, can't get caught here. What if...Nubbin pulls up lame? He'd come back. Elder Purdy sick? No preacher. Back early. Kill me where I'm laying. Her too. He pulled his arm from under her shoulders.

Startled, Tillie looked at him.

"I guess I'd better start work on that stall door," he said and rolled to the edge of the bed. *What if he got sick? Kill us both like this. Better get to the barn.*

"We've got plenny of time yet, Luke," she said and sat up holding the bedcovers at her throat.

"It's a purty big chore," he said and hunched on the side of the bed and pulled on his britches, his back to her, hiding his nakedness, not looking at hers.

Is that it? No more wanting? Eyes like a begging hound dog, groan, moan then no more needing, no more wanting. She frowned at his bent back and slipped her nightgown over her head and buttoned it, carefully matching button to buttonhole.

“I guess you had,” she said.

“I’ll get started,” he said. He stood up and glanced at her with a quick smile and walked from the room, his shoelaces untied.

His brogans clopped up the dogtrot, over the kitchen floor and across the porch. *Didn’t take time to tie his shoes*! The lot gate thwacked shut. She sat on the side of the bed and slipped her feet into her shoes. She touched her hair. *Guess I’m a sight.*

Swinging her feet off the bed, she got up and pulled the sheets tight and fluffed his pillows, the smell and taste of him in her nostrils and in her mouth. He’d wanted her, then, but not now. He left with his head hanging, no parting kiss. He didn’t even look at her.

Is this the way it is? Is it always this way? Wanting, giving, taking, being one, then shame and no more wanting? It’s got to be more than this. She spread the quilt and smoothed it over his bed. *There’s got to be more*! Abruptly, she straightened from making the bed and hurried from the room and followed him out the back door. She had to know if he still wanted her as much as she still needed his wanting. She lifted her nightgown from her flailing legs, and the morning chill swirls round her calves and thighs. She ran into the horse sweat and dung effluvium of the barn, and when he saw her, he straightened from the stall door and dropped the hammer to the ground.

Chapter Eleven

Under the late winter sun, the congregation flowed from the church house and clotted into chattering groups in the churchyard. Matt stood alone and watched Thurston give Retty a hand up onto their wagon.

"Brother Matt, you tell Sister Tillie that we're praying for her," Sister Purdy said.

Taking off his hat, Matt turned to her voice.

"I surely will, Sister Purdy," Matt said. "I think this long winter is most of her complaint." He smiled as Elder Purdy shook his hand.

"Well, Brother Matt," he said. "I didn't have a chance to tell you earlier, but I'm proud to tell you that Brother Horace Odom nominated you for deacon with no opposition. We'll hold the election of deacons during our July meeting."

"If I'm approved, God willing, Elder Purdy, I'll do my best for the church with the Lord's help." Matt felt a surge of pride and vindication that he had been nominated and without opposition. Thurston could have objected.

"I know you will," Elder Purdy said. "We're needin' young hearts and heads like yours in our leadership."

"Pardon us, Elder Purdy," Horace said and extended his hand to Matt. "Bertie and I wanna congratulate Matt and ask about Tillie."

"Thank you for nominating me, Brother Horace and like I told Sister Purdy, I think most of Tillie's complaint is a long winter."

"I think we can all sympathize with that," Bertie said. And they laughed.

"Pardon me, folks," Matt said. "But I wanna have a word with Thurston before he gets off."

"Go ahead, Brother Matt," Elder Purdy said. "I need a word with Brother Horace while I've got him here."

Matt walked hurriedly to Thurston's wagon. Retty and the girls sat in their chairs in the wagon bed. Asa sat on the front seat as Thurston slowly climbed the wheel spokes to sit beside him and took up the reins.

"I was sorry to hear about you gittin' hurt, Thurston," Matt said looking up at him. "You know I'm more than willing to give you a hand anytime."

"I appreciate your offer Matt," Thurston said. "Say, I unnerstand you and Tillie took Luke in."

"Yeah, we did, Thurston. The boy came to our place cold and hungry and said he didn't have no place to go, so we took him in."

"You know y'all ain't doing right, Matt, you know that I didn't free him," Thurston said. "And I need him to help me out on the place."

"I wouldn't have felt right about turning him away, Thurston. I figured he'd just go somewhere else. Maybe leave the country."

"You're wrong, Matt. Dead wrong. You ain't doing the boy no favor."

Matt looked at Retty. She smiled and nodded.

"Gee around, mules. Gee up!"

The mules leaned into harness, and the wagon rolled out of the churchyard into the Buskin Road. Matt watched until the wagon rounded the first bend in the road before he set his hat on his head and walked to his horse.

*

As Matt rode up the lane toward the house, Luke walked from the barn to the front gate.

"How's that stall door swinging now, old son?" Matt said. Smiling he stepped down from the saddle.

"It'll do." Luke looked back toward the barn. "I'll unsaddle Nubbin and see to him, Matt. You go on in the house."

"I'm obliged," Matt said and handed Luke the reins. "How's Tillie feeling?"

"Fine, I guess," he said. "When I went in to stoke the fire 'bout an hour ago, she was up and stirring, and I fetched her a drink of water."

"Good," Matt said. "I talked to your pa after church." He tried to catch Luke's eyes.

"How're the folks doing? How's Pa?" Luke asked, and glancing at Matt, he wondered, *What can he see in my eyes? Did what me and Tillie do show in my eyes? Can Matt see it in my eyes*? He looked to make sure that his shirt was tucked in, and turning his back to Matt, he raised the stirrup iron and ringed it on the pommel.

"They're all well, now, but your pa was down a coupla days last week after he hung a plow point on a root, and it jerked one of the handles into his ribs. Bruised him up purty bad, but he's up and kicking now."

"Durn," Luke said. "He always did plow at a fast trot, even in new ground. But he's alright now?" He talked with his back to Matt as he loosened the cinch strap, thinking Matt knew something was amiss, but he just hadn't figured out what, yet.

"Seems to me like he is. Are you gonna unsaddle Nubbin here at the front gate?" Matt said and chuckled.

"I was just loosening the girth," he said. "I figured to give him an easy breath."

"Suit yourself. I'm going on in the house." Matt stopped and turned inside the gate and said, "By the way, old son, you might oughta give him a ear of corn."

"Sure enough, Matt," Luke said and led the horse toward the barn.

Tillie sat in front of the dresser mirror running a comb through her hair. She smiled at him in the glass when he entered their bedroom and tossed his hat on the neatly made bed.

"Looks to me like you got a little of your color back, Tillie. Did your head get easy?" He leaned to her, and she offered her cheek for his kiss.

"Oh yeah, and as soon as I get my hair up, I'm gonna start fixing early supper. None of us has ate much today."

"Old Luke might make a doctor yet." He loosened his tie and unbuttoned the stiff collar.

"If toting water and stoking the cookstove's all it takes to make a doctor," she said. "What came out of the deacons meeting?"

"Elder Purdy told me that my name was put up for deacon and approved." He smiled at her in the mirror.

"Oh, Matt," she said, and standing, she hugged him. "I'm sure you'll be elected."

"Elder Purdy seems to think so, and he preached a fine sermon."

"What did he preach about?"

"The parable of the good Samaritan. I guess it was about as fine a sermon as I ever heard him preach."

"I regret I missed hearing him," she said. "Did you talk to Retty and Thurston?"

"Yeah, I spoke with 'em after church. Seems Brother Horace was right. Thurston was down a couple days, but he's fine now."

"Did he mention Luke?"

"Yeah, he said we wa'n't doing Luke no favor by taking him in."

"I'm mighty glad to hear he's fine," she said. "But it sounds to me like he may've slept through another sermon."

*

At the supper table, Luke's gaze shifted from his plate to the lamp, then to the red and white flowers in the table oilcloth. He slowly forked up small portions from his plate.

"You don't seem to have much appetite this evening, old son," Matt said. "That stall door didn't wear you out, did it?"

"What? No. No just feeling a little tired. May be catching what Tillie's got." He lowered his eyes into his plate.

"I sure hope not," Matt said and grinned at Tillie. She raised her eyebrows in a shrug.

"I suppose I'm just tuckered out, Matt. I think I'll go on to bed early."

He rose from the table and carried his plate to the back porch and raked the scraps into the yard for the hounds. Coming back into the kitchen, he set the plate on the washstand.

"I'll see y'all in the morning," he said.

"Let us know if you get to feeling worse, old son," Matt said.

They listened as he walked up the dogtrot and closed the bedroom door.

"I hope Luke ain't really caught something," Matt said. "I noticed he seemed outta sorts when I came in from church but fixing that stall door oughtn't to have worn him out."

"No. Course it didn't, Matt," she said, her voice lowered. "I figure he's a little bit homesick. He talked about Retty and the young'uns today, and I think he's feeling guilty about leaving home the way he did."

"Well, I hope that's all it is," Matt said. "If Thurston hadn't been so durn hard on him, he probably wouldn't have left in the first place."

"That's so, and I think he's feeling guiltier after hearing about Thurston gittin' hurt. Let's just not watch him so close. You know, if you feel bad about something and folks get to watching you, you start to actin' like you've really done something wrong even when you ain't." She patted his wrist and rose. "If you're through with supper I'll clear the table and wash the dishes."

*

Under the quilts, Luke curled and sank into the feather mattress, his body slowly warming the bed. He heard their voices and the clack of plates. *Tillie washing dishes. Matt sitting at the table talking to her. What's he saying? Asking? What's she telling? Couldn't help it. She should've said no. Could've. I didn't make her. He musta seen it in my eyes, my face. Not hers. No. Not hers. She talked and acted just like nothing happened. Wake up in the morning. Dreamed it. Durn, she wanted it as much as me! Come out in the cold. Ran to the barn. Matt kept asking me about that durn stall door! Can he see it in my face? My eyes?*

A door opened and closed, and voices died in the cold distance.

Gone to bed? Will she do it with him now? If he wants to, I hope she does. Don't rowel him. get him to thinking. Maybe it's alright. Durn.

The cook fire died, and the iron stove clanked and popped as it cooled, and the boards in the walls and the joists under the floor, pulled by the cold, crept and groaned. Faint footfalls slowly tiptoed in the dogtrot, passed his bedroom, and going up the dogtrot, they stopped at the front door. The house settled into the cold night, and the sounds ceased.

Bracing himself with his feet and shoulders, he turned onto his back without leaving the warm dent his body had pressed into the feather mattress. He stared into the darkness, thinking, *Eyes black as chinquapins. Leah Tupper's eyes. She let me touch her breasts. Like holding a quail, warm, soft, in my palm. Then pushed me away. Old man Tupper. Leah's pa. Bill Tupper. Indian? Says we're cousins. Pa says no. Old man took a liking to Pa when he was a boy. Shooting ducks and fishing on Nashobee Lake. Tillie. God! Her eyes ate a fellow up.*

He heard footsteps in the dogtrot again, even fainter this time. He held his breath and waited for them to tread pass his bedroom door. They stopped, and he heard the faint scratching of fingernails on wood, feeling for the doorknob. The door latch clicked, and he sat up in bed.

"Who's there?" he whispered; his voice hoarse.

"Ssh, It's me," Tillie said. And he felt the mattress sag as she climbed onto the bed. "Let me under the covers, Luke. It's cold."

"Where's Matt? What?" He threw the quilts back, and she crawled into the warm spot next to him. She shivered and pulled close.

"He's asleep, silly."

"I don't know about this, Tillie."

"Hush. I wanna talk to you." She curled her knee over his thighs, pressed a breast against his chest, and laid her mouth close to his ear. "Scrooch me up, Luke. I'm cold."

He turned on his side and hugged her to him and smelled the smoky, baked biscuit, female smell of her.

"That's better, sweetheart."

"What if he wakes up?"

"He won't wake up if the house falls off the blocks. You know that."

"I guess, but..."

"I wanted to tell you to not act sick or anything around Matt."

"I think he might suspect, Tillie. The way he looks at me."

"He don't suspect anything. He's just afraid you might be sick, the way you're actin'."

"Don't you love him, Tillie?"

"Matt's my husband, Luke, and I care for him very much. Don't ever think I don't. Ever. But he don't never study on this kinda thing."

"Never?"

"Seldom if ever. What we did won't ever bother him. He'll never find out. Besides, he don't like to do it."

"Damn!"

"Ssh. Don't cuss, Luke. Just act natural. He'll never know."

*

Tillie behaved as though nothing had happened between Luke and her. She touched Matt often and in the same manner as she always had. In Luke's presence and alone, she stroked his shoulder or lightly touched his hand or wrist, almost fawning.

Luke continued in his quietness and refused to look Matt in the eye or to look at Tillie in Matt's presence.

"I don't know what's wrong with that boy," Matt said. "He won't perk up."

"I think it's time you had a talk with him, Matt," Tillie said. "You know he blames hisself about Thurston gittin' hurt. Talk to him and tell him it ain't his fault."

That evening, Matt brought it up to Luke in the barn while they milked and fed the stock.

"Luke," he said. "You gonna have to quit blaming yourself about what happened."

Luke's back was to Matt, and his hands paused on Belle's teats. *Durn, she told*! His face burned and if he hadn't been sitting on the milking stool, his knees would have folded.

"Your pa's a stubborn man," Matt said. "And more 'n likely if you hadn't mentioned anything to him about him freeing you, he would've been trying to get shed of you by now, probably before you did leave."

Luke took a deep breath and nodded his head. Relief rippled through his muscles from his face to his knees. He squeezed Belle's teats and stifled a sudden urge to laugh.

"I guess you're right about that, Matt," he said and looked over his shoulder at him.

"I am," Matt said. "Now, you perk up and quit mullin' this thing so much. Thurston's doing fine, and you got a home here with me and Tillie as long as need be."

"I'm obliged, Matt."

"Finish the milking, and let's head on up to the house, old son," Matt said and slapped him on the shoulder. "Tillie's got supper on the table by this time."

And slowly, the secret of his coupling with Tillie became no more of a burden to bear than any of the other secret musings of lust or thoughts of anger and envy that he hid. He became used to the hidden life he lived under Matt's roof, and he and Matt returned to their easy banter. Luke jumped at every chance to tease him about his failure to catch anything more in his traps than a few coons and rabbits.

"Looks to me like you need to commence trying to remember all them things you learnt me about trapping and then forgot," he said.

"I'll catch us plenny of cash hides before the season's out, old son," Matt said. "You just take care of the milking and keep plenny of firewood on hand for Tillie."

They laughed at their joshing, but Tillie said, "You're gonna end up eating your words, Luke Knox. Trapping ain't over yet, and there's been times when Matt made more money from coon and mink hides than a lot of folks made on their cotton crops."

Chapter Twelve

In early April, the dogwoods and hawthorns bloomed, and the white smears of blossoms bleeding through the gray, somber woods augured the end of trapping.

"First thing this morning, Luke, we'll start rowing up the corn patch and see if we can't get it ready to plant by the end of the week," Matt said. "Then we'll split firewood and set up the wash pot. Tillie tells me she's got behind with her washing."

Luke nodded at Matt over his coffee cup.

"This afternoon, I guess I'd best take up my traps," he said.

"You want me to give you hand?" Luke said.

"If you don't mind, old son, I wish you'd stay and tote water for Tillie and give her a hand with the washing."

"Not a-tall," Luke said. He grinned at Tillie, then Matt. "Why, I suspect you caught might near enough cash hides to buy another steel trap for next season."

Matt guffawed and shook his head.

"Now don't you set in, Luke," Tillie said. "It's just been a poor season. Besides, there's been times when Matt…"

"I know, Tillie," Luke said. "I recall times when Matt made more on hides than a lot of folks made on their cotton, too, but I hope that don't hold true this year."

"I hope it too, old son," Matt said and scraped back his chair from the table and rose. "I sure hope folks make more on cotton than we did on hides this year."

*

Early in the afternoon, Matt saddled Nubbin and set off to take up his traps. Luke drew water from the well and began filling the iron wash pot. Tillie walked to the kitchen backdoor and watched Matt ride into the woods beyond the barn lot. Luke glanced over his shoulder, and seeing Tillie turning back into the kitchen, he let go of the well rope. The pulley whined as the draw-bucket fell and splashed in the bottom of the well. Hurrying to the house, he mounted the porch in two steps. In the kitchen, Tillie slid two raisin pies into the oven. Luke stepped behind her and wrapped her in his arms.

"Not yet, Luke, I've got pies in the oven. I don't wanna burn them."

"My God, Tillie, I'm burning!" His hands cuddled her breasts, urgent, insistent.

She leaned her head back on his chest and savored the familiar tightening of her loins and turned in his arms. With her head tilted back, and her eyes half closed, she saw a shadow fall through the open kitchen door.

"Don't, Luke!" A terrible weakness swept from the pit of her stomach into her arms and legs, and she pushed from him and slapped his hand. "Behave yourself! Go draw the wash water!"

Luke stepped back, his mouth agape, trying to catch her eye, but she looked at Matt in the kitchen door. For a moment, Matt's face was blank, his eyes not quite focused, then his eyebrows puckered, and his mouth pulled thin and sour.

Luke turned.

"What the--?" Matt said.

Luke broke into a run for the hall door on the other side of the kitchen.

"Durn you, boy! I seen what you did!"

"No, Matt!" Tillie grabbed the crook of his elbow as he lunged for Luke, and Luke slipped through the door and ran through the hall.

"I'll break your neck, boy!" Matt said. Again, he tried to follow, but she clung to his arm with both hands. "Run as far and as fast as you can, boy! I'm gonna put a ball in your brains, you durn rapscallion you!"

"Matt!" Tillie's heart thumped, and she stepped between him and the door. Luke's feet pounded across the front porch, and the gate slammed shut.

"He's just a boy, darling!" Tillie said. She squeezed his wrist and pulled him closer to her. "You're a full-grown man. get a hold of yourself, sweetheart. You know how boys can get outta hand sometimes."

"It looked to me like he was more than outta hand," he said. "Has he pulled anything like that before?" The tendons in his neck corded.

"Why, no. Of course not! Look at me, Matt. Don't you know I would've told you if he had? I'm your wife, darling."

Matt felt a sudden rush of guilt for having asked her such a question. His chest swelled as he took a deep breath. He let it out with a long sigh, and the grimace faded from his face as he calmed.

"I scolded him," she said and nodded toward the front door, then looked up into Matt's face. "And it's a certainty he heard how you feel about it. Let's not make a big row over it, not make any more of it than what it really is."

"I would've thought Luke had more respect for you and for me than to try and pull something like that," he said. His hand trembled as he wiped it across his mouth.

"He's just a big ole boy, darling," she said. Moving closer, she slipped her arm round his waist and stroked his side. "It's got nothing to do with respect. You're a big, ole grown man, but he's just a big, ole curious boy feeling his oats."

He put his arm around her shoulders and hugged her to him.

"By gads," he said. "He'd better be particular about whose oats it is he's feeling from here on out."

"And not your oats, my darling?"

"That's the idee," he said. Then, he chuckled and shook his head. "Confound that boy."

"I'm yours, sweetheart and only yours," she said and pressing against him, she drew his hand from her shoulder to her breast. "I am yours, Matt. Don't you know that, darling. I want to have your babies. I want us to have our family." His fingertips gently stroked. "I want us to have lots and lots of babies."

"Tillie, you know how I can be." His heart pounded.

"I'm your wife, sweetheart." Her hand covered his and pressed it on her breast. "We're supposed to be one. Scripture tells us that."

"I'm afraid I'll hurt you, darling."

"No, no. You won't hurt me, sweetheart," she said, leading him into their bedroom. "We'll learn together, how to be one."

She stood in front of him at the side of their bed.

With trembling fingers, he unbuttoned her dress front. He missed a button and went back, and the dress opened from the neck to below her waist, and he pushed it off her shoulders. She raised her arms, and he drew her chemise over her head. His loins and the small of his back wilted with a strange pleasure, and a groan rose in his throat. His chest heaving, eyes wide with a wanting of her, he pulled and pushed his coat, shirt and britches, dropping them to the floor.

"Let's make a baby, sweetheart," she said, and lying on the bed, she slipped her thumbs under the waistband of her drawers and pushed them to her knees. He pulled them from her legs, and warm and open, she clung to him and gasped.

"Did I hurt…?"

"No, no. It's wonderful!" She hugged his neck, roughly pulling him to her, and arching up to him, she sobbed.

And possessing and yielding, they demanded and relinquished until the bitter smell of burning raisin pies flooded the bedroom. She struggled beneath him.

"Let me up, sweetheart, quick!" She pushed on his shoulders.

He looked at her, his face fearful, and rolled from her.

"Did I hurt you, Tillie? I…"

"No, my sweetheart." She slipped from the bed, her knees trembling. "Your pies, my love! Your favorite. I burnt your raisin pies!"

He pawed for the quilt to cover his nakedness, but she laughed, giggled and pulled it from him.

"I'll be back directly," she said, and clutching the quilt around her naked shoulders, she ran into the smoke-filled kitchen.

Chapter Thirteen

Switch cane and briars and hawthorn and wax myrtle shrubs tangled either side of the cutoff trail. When he reached the foot log that crossed Hennessey Creek, Luke stopped running.

Durn her! She made it look like it wa'n't her doing, like she didn't want it.

Sweat slid from his wind-matted hair and streaked his face and burned his eyes. He bent, his hands braced on his knees, and his breath heaved, deeply, rapidly. His heart pounded. He raised his head and peered through laced sunlight breaking through the limbs of oak and beech and the taller cypress trees, back up the cutoff trail toward Matt's place.

Hidden in the silence, an Indianhead woodpecker cackled loudly then suddenly ceased.

She'll tell him ever'thing. He straightened and looked down the cutoff trail toward Seth's place, then at the cold current in the creek, his mouth sticky with thirst. *Damn, he'll be in the saddle and comin' after me, but I've gotta have a swig of water.*

He jogged stiff-legged down the steep embankment into the creek bed. The creek was waist deep here and easily crossed on horseback, but he wasn't going to wade. Dropping to his knees, he leaned forward on his hands, forearm deep in the cold water. Beneath the wavering image of his eyes staring back at him, he saw the sandy bottom like rippled clouds. He muzzled his image and drank. The water tasted fresh, woody with a bitter edge. He drank again and sitting back in the sand, he wiped his wet shirtsleeve across his face. His breath came slower, but deep and steady.

"Damn!" The single word cracked the quiet murmur of the creek. *Damn her hide, she's done told him how I mounted her ever'time he left the house. Damn! He's killing mad for certain and got his gun and saddled up by now.* Standing, he scrabbled on hands and feet to the high bank and peered back down the cutoff trail toward Matt's place.

Gotta hurry. He's on Nubbin and riding, by now. He turned and stepped out on the foot log, and with his arms floating up from his sides for balance, he quick-stepped across to the far bank. He looked back once more and held his breath, listening intently, trying to hear the pounding of hoofs. A cat squirrel squealed then barked in the woods north of the trail, and a mockingbird cock whistled and chirped but no sound of hoof-beats. Not yet.

He'll figure I'm headed for Seth's, and what the hell can Seth do for me? I'll just get him killed, too. I'm gonna have to light a shuck outta here, maybe to Nashobee Lake or Clemson, to Aunt Hannah and Uncle Lee's. Can't go to Seth.

And he set out in a trot along the trail then pushed harder until he was in a run. As his pace fell into rhythm, his thoughts became nothing more than pounding hooves and horse sweat and flared nostrils and the sour, cruel twist of Matt's anger. A quarter mile and he came to a break in the south edge of the trailside tangle.

I can't go to Seth's place. And he cut through the gap into the woods. Under the shade of hardwood and cypress, scattered holly and yaupon and hawthorn shrubs struggled for light and life, and Luke slowed to a walk and took his bearings on the sun. Coursing with the afternoon sun high on his right shoulder, he headed south.

But Clemson or Nashobee Lake ain't neither one far enough. He'll find out where I am in a week's time. I'm gonna have to get plumb outta the country, head for Texas. To Uncle Doss and Aunt Mavis. By the time he finds out I'm there, I'll be gone to Indian Territory or California. Durn her.

Through the woods, he held his course by habit, without thought, dimly aware of twigs snapping underfoot and birds calling in the branches overhead.

And if I circle round through the swamp, I can get home before he finds out I didn't go to Seth's. At least I can tell Ma and Pa and the young'uns bye before I light out for Texas. He pushed between a holly and hawthorn shrub and forged ahead until briar vines caught him across his chest and snared and scratched his ankles.

"Damn! Tarnation, and hellfire!"

He looked round but couldn't see beyond the hawthorn shrubs, cross briars, vines, and switch cane that had swallowed him up.

"Walked right dab in the middle of a damn thicket," he said aloud.

Damn. Gotta work my way outta this briar patch. Fool! Watch where you're going.

He unhooked briar thorns from his shirt and britches and high-stepped over briars and vines, following the twists and turns of what looked to be a rabbit or raccoon trail through the thicket. Finally going down on all fours, he crawled along the dim path.

Hope old buzz tail ain't nosing around in here, too. As his senses heightened, he smelled the musty leaf mold and heard a wren flush from the thicket, chittering. He struggled against the primal fear coiled in the tan and brown and darker leaves and the tawny cat's tail curling across his brain and crawled until the undergrowth thinned, and he dragged himself clear of the thicket and stood and looked around to take his bearings. The ground swelled and rose in front of him. He looked around, trying to find his bearings. At his back, the sun perched in the rose-colored budding oak branches.

This can't be the high bank of the Hennessey, he thought. *If it is, I'm on the west bank and that can't be. I couldn't have crossed the creek and not seen it.*

He walked up on the rise to look beyond it and looked down into the creek bed. Quickly, he glanced back at the sun, then into the creek. It flowed to his left!

"That can't be," he mumbled. "It's running north! The Hennessey runs south, and anyhow, I couldn't be on the west bank without I crossed the creek, and I ain't crossed the confounded creek since I left the cutoff trail."

His senses were stunned, but he knew he must be within five miles of either Seth's or Matt's place or home. He looked across the creek into the strange, unfamiliar woods, and tilting his head, he listened for the barking of a dog or the crowing of a rooster, but no domestic sound broke the rushing silence. Small birds whistled and chittered.

His throat tightened, and he remembered the morning of the coon hunt when they had heard a panther squall within a quarter mile of them. *Tracks big as hoof prints*. He slipped his hand into his pocket and grasped his Barlow knife. The roof of his mouth tasted sharp and metallic, and a chill slid between his shoulder blades. He shivered and looked up stream. The creek flowed from the thicket.

I ain't goin back in there, he thought. *Lost! Lord, I can't be lost. Damn! How'd I get on the west bank? I'll have to follow the creek out though, until I find myself.* He turned and walked along the high bank, downstream, the thicket at his back and the sun on his left shoulder. *Walking downstream the creek should be running south and the sun should be on my right*. His ears tuned to every rustle and stir. *Gotta find myself. Matt can come riding up anytime now*. He pushed down an urge to break into a run and cast his eyes from side to side through the woods, trying to locate some familiar rise in the ground or maybe a known turkey roost. *Or was it really morning when I ran from Matt. If it was, that means the sun's in the east and the creek's running south like it ought to. No. Hell, no. It wa'n't morning. It was afternoon. Tillie had put pies in the oven to bake for supper. I remember that, certain. Durn her! I can't be lost! But I don't know where the hell I am, and that's lost, old son, sure as shooting.*

He glanced up, and the sun now shined in his face. He quickly looked to his left and saw the thicket through the open woods. His heart leapt as he recognized the woods.

"Now I see," he said aloud. "'I once was blind, but now I see!'"

He walked faster, following the creek. It rounded a long curve until he headed back toward the thicket. The creek ran south now, and he recognized the twenty-foot-tall snag of a lightning-deadened cypress tree. His senses quickened as the stump and the woods around it became familiar.

I once was lost.

Ten or twelve years ago, a windstorm snapped the dead cypress, and it fell and broke the hardwoods beneath it, opening an acre or more of ground. Over the years, the thicket grew up and entangled the clearing.

"Hellfire! But 'now I'm found!'"

He was inside one of the many large double-back loops the creek made in its meandering course. He had crawled through the neck of the loop as he worked his way out of the thicket, the cypress butt on his left and the creek's high banks on his left and right, hidden by the dense thicket of cane and briars. He almost shouted with joy at finding himself then realized he was only a little better than a mile south of the cutoff trail.

Hurriedly, he sat and slipped off his brogans, tied the laces together and stuffed his socks into the shoes. Peeling off his shirt, then his britches and drawers, he rolled them into a bundle and slung his brogans over his shoulder. Naked, he picked his way among roots and cypress knees down the embankment into the creek. The cold water stung the briar cuts on his ankles and legs. He took a deep breath and lifted his roll of clothes onto his head and stepped out into the cold current. His calves and thighs quivered as he waded, waist-deep then chest-deep. The soles of his brogans dipped into the cold water that wrapped his body. His breath came hard and short. Sliding one foot ahead of the other, he felt the soft, uncertain creek bottom with his bare feet, making sure of firm step before he pulled the other foot forward. As his weight shifted, the leaf-matted creek bed gave, sinking under his foot, and air bubbles rushed up and swirled around his ankles and calves before the current swept them downstream. He slowly waded, crossed the depth and began emerging from the water, waist-deep, calf-deep, then naked and cold on the bank.

"G-g-god-d-damn!"

To keep his teeth from popping together, he clamped his mouth closed so tight his jaw muscles ached, and carefully, he climbed up through roots and cypress knees to the high bank. His body shivered and jerked. The broken, branch-laced sunshine felt as radiant as a stove on his chill-tight skin.

Only five more miles to home, old son. You can make it that far naked in a hailstorm.

Briskly, he wiped the water from his chest and belly and legs with his shirt and drawers and put them on. Holding his britches by the waistband, he shook them out in front of him and stiff-kneed his left foot, then his right through the legs.

Only five miles, five more miles.

He sat in the leaf mold and brushed the sand and twigs from the soles of his feet. He pulled on his socks, and then his brogans and tied the laces and pushed himself to his feet.

Chapter Fourteen

Trudging against the afternoon sun, Thurston followed the plow and mule and watched the sandy loam flow over the wing of the turning plow. He figured in another half-day, another day at the most, he would finish rowing his ten acres of new ground as well as his twenty-acre cotton field. At the turn-row, he reined the mule around and set the plow point to continue making the next row. Taking a deep breath, he felt a slight pull in his ribs.

He had objected when Retty sent Joe Burgess to fetch Dr. Foley, but he was glad for it now.

"Come up, Jack," he said, setting the mule in motion.

His objection had turned to irritation when he walked from his barn chores that evening and saw Dr. Foley's gray horse tied at the side gate. Dr. Foley was almost seventy years old, a widower, and a couple of years older than Thurston's pa and had served in the War with his pa and his uncles. After the War, he earned his medical degree in New Orleans. Thurston's younger sister was scared of the old doctor, but most folks along the Hennessey Creek thought him a Godsend.

When Thurston entered the kitchen-house with the evening milk, he saw Dr. Foley sitting at the table drinking coffee. A full gray beard covered his face. He sipped his coffee from a saucer then raked the knuckle of his forefinger under his wet mustache.

"I unnerstand you got a crack in the ribs, Thurston," Dr. Foley said.

"Retty's making a fuss about nothing, Doc Foley," he said and lifted the milking pail onto the kitchen shelf. "Nothing but bruised ribs." He hung his hat and coat from nails on the back of the door.

"I want you to give him a good going over, Dr. Foley," Retty said. "He's been dragging around here like a foundered mule all spring, and I want you to fix him up."

"Well, let's go over in the house, Thurston," Dr. Foley said. "I'll give you a thorough examination." And he picked up his worn, black medical bag and led the way out the kitchen-house door.

In the big front room, Thurston stripped to the waist and sat on a straight chair near a front window. Dr. Foley settled on a chair next to him and set his bag on the floor.

"Let me have a look at those ribs," he said. He leaned toward Thurston and gently pressed the large, purplish bruise. "Looks like you whacked yourself purty hard."

Thurston grunted and winced under Dr. Foley's probing.

"Well, it may've cracked a rib or two, but they're not broke. Retty tells me she's been rubbing you with liniment."

"Ever' evening, Doc."

"I can't recommend anything more 'n that," he said. "Now, what's ailing you, Thurston? Retty knows something's amiss with you."

"Well, Doc, I ain't let on to Retty, didn't wanna worry her, and I don't want you to let on to her what I tell you, but I had a spell with my heart last fall, and I'm afraid I won't last till pickin' time."

"Huh," Dr. Foley grunted and taking Thurston's wrist in his hand felt his pulse. "What kinda spell?"

"I got plumb dizzy," Thurston said. "Thought I was gonna faint dead-away. I had to grab ahold to my wagon to keep from falling."

Dr. Foley nodded as Thurston talked.

"Well, your pulse is a strong, steady sixty-two." He released Thurston's wrist and reached his stethoscope from his bag. Hooking the instrument into his ears, he pressed the cone to Thurston's chest, then his back.

"Take a deep breath and hold 'er. Alright, breathe." He moved the cone to several spots on his back repeating his instructions on each move. "Alright, you can relax and breathe, now," he said and folded the tubes of his stethoscope and slipped it into his bag.

"What was you doing when you had this spell?"

"I was emptying a sack of cotton," he said. "We was 'bout finished pickin' for the day, and I hoisted my cotton sack onto the wagon bed to empty it, and I went plumb faint. My heart was beating hard and fast and I staggered like a drunk man."

"Where was your pain? Where did you hurt?"

"Well, I can't say as I had any particular pain, Doc. But I remember that Retty's pa had a coupla fainting spells before his heart gave out on him."

"I see," Dr. Foley said. "Have you had a spell since pickin' time?"

"No, can't say as I have, Doc, but I sure was weak for several days after," Thurston said. "And I've been particular to move purty ginger since then."

"As I recall, it was purty hot during cotton pickin' last year, right into November."

"That's a fact."

"How old are you, now, Thurston? Forty, Forty-five?"

"I turned forty-two in February."

"Your heart's as sound as a dollar as far as I can tell. Your lungs are clear as a bell, and you've got a strong, steady pulse," Dr. Foley said and ran his knuckle under his mustache. "You may drop dead when you stand up from that chair, and I may drop dead gittin' onto my horse out there, but ain't neither one of us ever had a spell with our heart 'til now."

"What do you think it was I had, Doc? How come I had that dizzy spell?"

"I think you got overheated, maybe even close to having a sunstroke. Don't try to do ever'thing on the place in one day, Thurston. You ain't a twenty-five-year-old lad anymore."

Thurston inhaled and slowly let his breath out.

"What do I owe you, Doc?"

"Put your shirt on and let's go out to the kitchen. Retty's gonna pay me with supper and a bowl of butter."

*

At the north edge of the field, Luke pressed his face against the rough bark of a large, sweetgum tree and watched his pa follow the plow and mule for a long time before he stepped out and walked across the field, his brogans sinking into the raw, newly turned dirt.

Thurston saw him and pulled the mule to a halt and wrapped the lines around the plow handle. He took off his hat and wiped his brow with his shirtsleeve.

"Howdy, Pa."

"Well, I see you come home without your hat and coat, son," Thurston said. "What's them scratches on your face? You been fighting a wildcat?"

"No sir, Pa. I got tangled up in a thicket coming through the swamp." Luke dropped his eyes as Thurston looked closely at his face. "I come to say my good-byes to you and Ma and the young'uns."

"What kinda trouble you in, Luke?" His stomach tightening, he reset his hat on his head.

"Matt's after me, Pa. He's gonna kill me." He glanced back across the field as though he expected to see Matt.

Thurston spat into the dirt, wiped his hand over his mustache, and nodded his head. *Two young men and one young woman under one roof sounds like the kind of trouble that could get a fellow killed.*

"I told Matt he oughtn't to have taken you in. He done wrong there, putting in between me and mine. What happened with y'all?"

"Well, Pa," he said, his voice low. "It's kinda hard to say." He rubbed the back of his neck with his hand and looked over his shoulder again.

"It's hard to say because you're not sure what happened, or it's hard to say because you're ashamed to say the words?"

"Yes sir. I guess that's it," Luke said. "I'm sure what happened, I just don't wanna say the words."

"I'll suspect Tillie figures in all this."

"Yes sir. She does."

Thurston looked toward the kitchen-house.

"Luke, have you been laying with Tillie?"

"Yes sir, I guess so." He glanced up expecting to see fire and wrath in his pa's face, but his eyes were calm and held a distant look, like he was calculating in his head how many pounds of cotton seed it'd take to plant the new ground.

"Did Tillie tell, or did Matt catch y'all?"

"He caught us, Pa. Right in the kitchen."

"In the kitchen? Was you laying with her in the kitchen?"

"No sir. We was just kinda hugging and such when he walked in, and Tillie seen him and pushed me away like she didn't like it anymore."

"So, Matt didn't see y'all laying together?"

"No sir, Pa. The way he acted seeing me hugging her, I figure he would've already shot me if he'd seen us laying together."

"Yeah, son," Thurston said. "I suspect he would've, but you go on up to the house and let your ma know you've come back home, but don't say nothing about having troubles over at Matt's place."

"But I'm gonna have to clear out, Pa. I'm heading for Texas. To Uncle Doss. Matt's coming after me. He's gonna kill me sure as—as sunrise."

"What makes you think your Uncle Doss'll take you in after you been laying with his brother's wife?" Thurston said.

"Why, he ain't heard about it yet."

"Do you figure a house plunderer afoot can beat the U. S. mail to Texas?"

"Matt won't know where I'm gone to."

"You don't think he won't be over here tomorrow or the day after, asking me and your ma where you're at?"

"Y'all don't have to tell him." Luke looked at his pa. His face was calm, and Luke thought, *Durn, he will though.*

"Luke, you wanted to be free," Thurston said. "And you've been free of this household nigh on to two months, and it appears to me like you ain't very free. You wouldn't mind me then run off and left me tellin' you I needed your help 'til pickin' time. You plundered the house of the man who took you in, your ma's own brother, and now you're asking honest folk to lie for you. You know, Luke, a feller can have enough money to burn a wet mule, but if he's a liar and a thief, has no character, nobody trusts him. He's got no sun or true star to course on. He just ambles from here to there to yonder, depending on whatever it is he dreads or lusts after. He's no freer than a buck chasing a doe in the rut. Without moral character nobody's free. The meanest and strongest and slyest would take and do whatever the lust of their peckers or their maws urged them to take and do, and the rest'd hide in holes like ground terrapins. I'm afraid you ain't learned much under my roof."

"I figure I did, Pa. I learned enough about right and wrong to unnerstand that I made a bad mistake, but I don't figure I oughta be killed for it."

"No, you oughtn't be killed for it, Luke, but a man's gotta know enough about right and wrong to unnerstand that making bad mistakes and not facing 'em down is what makes a liar and a coward out of him. Lying and cowardice is bondage and the worst kinda bondage. A coward lies, and a liar cows. Decency and grit's what makes a man free."

"I unnerstand that..."

"No, I don't think you do, Luke, and I want you to hear me out, whether you leave or stay." Thurston rubbed the fishhook-shaped scar on his knuckle, looked down at his hand, then said, "I want you to unnerstand that being free don't mean you're at liberty to walk in another man's house and take his goods just because you're sly enough or big enough to do it, and it don't mean you're allowed to lay with another man's wife just because she's willing and y'all can out fox her husband. Being free ain't a matter of going and coming on the whim of every yen and lust that winnows in your heart or maw. It's a matter of abiding by the rules of common decency, of bein' trusted and respected whenever and wherever you go or bide."

"Yes sir. I wish I could take it back," Luke said. "Wisht I'd never done it."

For a moment, he looked at Luke without speaking. He knew the boy regretted what he had done, but he knew that any fellow was apt to be repentant when the man he's offended is out to kill him.

"I regret I did such, Pa. What else can I say?"

"You can't say more 'n what you've said, Luke, but being regretful ain't enough. You're of an age when most folks make a choice. You're gonna have to choose whether you wanna be an honest man and walk upright in your goings and comings or whether you wanna be common and low-class. You think over what I've said. You have to choose."

Luke hung his head, and Thurston watched him until he looked up.

"Well, you go on up to the house and see your ma. Whether you go or stay is up to you, but if you live under my roof, and you're welcome, you're gonna abide by my rules."

"Yes sir. I wanna stay, Pa, but Matt's out to kill me, sure as, as—"

"Matt ain't gonna kill nobody, Luke," he said. "He's just mad. Can you blame him?"

"No sir," Luke said. "I can't blame him a-tall."

"Like I say, you go on up to the house but don't mention what happened over at Matt's to your ma or anybody else, ever."

"Yes sir, Pa," Luke said. He turned and walked across the raw dirt toward the house.

Thurston gripped the plow stock handles and chucked at the mule. He headed for the barn, thinking maybe Matt didn't know anything beyond what he'd seen in the kitchen and that Tillie was a smart enough girl not to tell him more, unless, somehow, it worked for her wellbeing to tell him more. What she may've told was the bind. He knew he'd have to talk to Matt and settle the matter about his threat to kill Luke, but he'd have to take care not to rouse Matt's suspicions that anything more happened than what he'd seen in the kitchen. It had to be put to rest, soon and now. Those kinds of words couldn't be left to fester and settle into Matt's feelings. But what should he say to Matt and how should he say it without telling him more than he already knew?

"Lord, have mercy on me a sinner." Thurston drew a long breath and thought, "*But if any provide not for his own, and especially for those of his own house, he hath denied the faith, and is worse than an infidel.*"

Chapter Fifteen

"Soon as you finish with your breakfast, Luke, I want you to saddle Button for me," Thurston said. "I'm gonna slip over to the pin oak flat on the other side of the Hennessey and see if I can't kill a turkey this morning."

"Yes sir, Pa," Luke said. He pushed back his chair and rose from the table.

"Finish your breakfast, son," Thurston said. "It's awhile till daylight."

"Can I go with you, Pa?" Asa said.

"Not this morning, son. One morning next week when we're caught up in the field, I'll get your Uncle Morgan to bring William over, and we'll all go turkey hunting."

"Kin I, Pa? Kin I go with you?" Callie said.

"No, sugar. You're gonna have to stay and help your ma and the girls."

"Why, Thurston," Retty said. "Are you setting off turkey hunting with work left in the field?"

"Me and Asa can feed and milk this morning, Ma," Luke said.

"Sure enough, Retty," Thurston said. "When a man's got sons on the place, he can take time to go turkey shooting now and again. Besides, I won't be gone but a coupla hours."

Though she chided him, she was pleased that his mood was lifted. After he had jabbed his side with the plow handle, a deep purple bruise blotched his ribs, and he could hardly get out of bed in the morning. The next Saturday, Joe Burgess came to call on Maud and when he left to go home, Retty sent word by him for Dr. Foley to come and examine Thurston the first time he came their way. Thurston had said he didn't need to pay Doc Foley to tell him that he had bruised ribs, and she snapped back that he wasn't going to pay him, she was and besides, he'd been moping around now going on half a year and she wanted the doctor to give him a good looking over. Luke's homecoming had been a lift to his spirits, too.

"Did you finish rowing the new ground yesterday?" Retty said.

"No, ma'am," Thurston said. "But Luke can have a good start to finishing by the time I get back."

Retty opened her mouth to speak again but saw he peered out the kitchen-house window, staring into the morning darkness. She'd lived with him long enough to know that when something lay heavy on his mind, he'd hold his peace until he had firmly gripped it himself before he'd tell her. He was anxious to get the new ground ready to plant, so the turkey hunt was his excuse to be by himself. She figured it must have to do with Luke and his coming home yesterday, but the Lord knew, he wouldn't tell her until he wrestled it to the ground, or it crippled him like Jacob's angel.

"Well, y'all better stir," she said and rose from the table. "By the time y'all get saddled, it'll be daylight. Maud, you fix the dish water, and Sarah, you can start clearing the table."

*

Luke swung open the lot gate, and with his heels, Thurston nudged Button through the gap.

"Good luck, Pa," Luke said.

Thurston silently touched the barrel of his rifle to his hat brim in answer and reined Button across the Buskin Road and entered the dark woods on a rut-worn stock path that fell in a long descent from the ridge to the nearest crossing on Hennessey Creek. A quarter moon set in the western sky giving little light, so he held the reins slack trusting Button to keep the trail. A light chill hung in the air, and a misty veil hugged the ground so that he saw tree trunks and shrubs at eye level more distinctly than he saw the path. Retty's rooster crowed at his back, and he knew he was riding due east toward the creek. He silently prayed for God's mercy in the matter that lay ahead of him. He believed and had faith that a man should expect goodness from the Lord's guidance, whether in great or small ventures. He was abroad upon a matter of great concern, a matter of providing for his own household. There had to be an end to it now. Harsh words left to fester turned to fear, to hate, and Matt was more than a younger brother-in-law. They had lived with Mr. Rufe not long after they married. Retty's ma died in childbirth, and they moved in with her pa, and she took care of Matt like he was her own. He slept in the bed with them, and he was only a year older than Seth and a couple of years older than Luke. The three had grown up like brothers.

He let Button have his head to follow the trail down the high bank to the creek. In little more than a mile, he crossed the stirrup-deep ford and climbed to the opposite high-bank.

"Whoa, Button," he said softly and stepped from the saddle and looped the bridle reins on the branch of a holly shrub. Cradling his rifle in the crook of his arm, he looked round the woods and up through the trees at the paling sky. Retty's rooster crowed, and sure of his bearings, he walked northeast soundlessly treading the damp leaf mold toward his usual stand at the base of a cypress tree.

At the edge of a pin oak flat, he backed against the butt of a cypress tree between two large ridges that ran from the ground and disappeared into the rounded trunk five feet above his head. Silently praying, he squatted, and his back slid noiselessly over the silky bark until he sat on the ground, his knees under his chin. He peered into the misty pin oak flat, and cupping his left hand over the receiver of his rifle to muffle the sound, he thumbed the hammer to full cock. Fishing his wing-bone call from his coat pocket, he slowly brought it to his lips.

As daylight broke, tree after tree separated from the darker woods until he clearly saw the trunk of the farthermost oak across the flat. A branch shook among the oaks, and another shook, and two, five, eight turkeys drifted to the ground and looked from side to side, their heads jerking, then scratched among the leaves, pecked, then raised their heads and looked round again. Their searching and pecking carried them away from him across the open flat. He made three yaps on his call, slipped it into his pocket, and raised the rifle to his shoulder, his elbows resting on his knees. A tom turned and walked toward him, stretched his neck. The loud gobble startled the woods as the notes bobbled from his throat. Scratching the ground throwing leaves and dirt, he pecked in the leaf mold then raised his head. The bare red and blue neck and waddles looked like melted candle wax running onto its bronze-copper breast. The beard drifted and waved from side to side in a light ground breeze, and the tom jerked his head side to side, looking, scratched, and ducked his head again.

Thurston aimed. The tom's head came up, jerked side to side; his eyes, glass beads and walked toward the cypress where Thurston sat and stopped and thrust his head up and forward. His mouth opened, and he gobbled again. Thurston held the front bead of the rifle in the rear buckhorn sight and settled it where the tom's naked head joined his neck. *Lord God, Be in the matter. Give me the right words.* He squeezed the trigger.

Orange flame spurted from the rifle muzzle into the gray morning. The sound of the blast rolled up and down Hennessey Creek. A sudden beating and flurry of heavy wings followed the gunshot, and branches waved and shook in the trees. A wisp of smoke hung in the air between him and the pin oak flat. The acrid smell of burnt gunpowder pierced his nostrils to the back of his tongue. The woods became silent. He lowered his head where he sat and for a long time, he continued to pray.

*

Thurston carried his rifle with the butt resting on his thigh as he rode out of the woods and struck the lane between Matt's house and his barn. He nudged Button's ribs with his heels and turned up the lane toward Matt who followed his mule and plow in his cornfield.

O Lord, I don't know how I oughta pray. Just give me the light. Gotta say the right words. Thy will be done. He didn't know how much Matt knew or how much Tillie had told him or how much he suspected. He hoped Tillie had calmed him whatever he knew or suspected. He reined Button into the ditch next to the rail fence, lowered his rifle across the saddle bow and sat and waited.

Lord knows. Luke was wrong. I know. But I gotta settle it, now.

Matt plowed up to the fence where Thurston waited and halted his mule.

"Morning, Thurston. How's Retty and the young'uns?" he said. He wrapped the lines around the plow stock handle and walked to the fence. Shading his eyes against the sun with his hand, he squinted up at Thurston.

"Tolerable," Thurston said. "You and Tillie?" He wiped his palm over his mustache, his eyes dark under his brows.

"Just fine," Matt said and nodded at the rifle. "I thought I heard somebody shoot down about the pin oak flat right after daylight."

"Yeah, it was me that shot. I missed him. I guess I'm going to have to start turkey shooting with a shotgun," Thurston said. "But the point of my visit is the trouble between you and Luke."

"The boy got outta line, Thurston," Matt said and frowned. "I ain't gonna put up with it."

"The boy was outta line the night he come to your place and y'all took him in. And when I spoke to you about it later, you was outta line when you said he was welcome to live at your place as long as he wanted to." He felt the keen edge of the words in his throat.

"He was welcome here as long as he showed respect for me and mine."

"I guess you know more 'n I do about what goes on in y'all's household, but he come home yesterday evening saying you aimed to kill him."

"He got outta line with Tillie."

"He told me how he acted with Tillie in the kitchen, and I straightened the boy out myself." His heart hammered. *Good God, boy. Don't argue. Gonna be settled here. Now. Can't leave it to fester.*

"We was mighty let down by Luke after all we'd done for him."

"I was mighty let down myself, Matt," Thurston's face reddened as he leaned forward in the saddle and looked Matt in the eye. "He told me you made a threat to kill him, but there's gotta be an end to it, now. You're Retty's brother, Matt, and I love you, but if you so much as lay a finger on a hair of that boy's head, there'll be a reckoning between me and you."

"There ain't no call for that kinda talk, Thurston," Matt said. Neither his eyes nor his voice wavered. "Ain't no call you saying such as that. He got outta line, and I was mad when I said it. I'm regretful I said such a thing, and it's forgot as far as I'm concerned."

Thurston sat back in the saddle, the high color slowly fading from his face. He raised the rifle barrel, touched it to the brim of his hat, and lowered it back across the saddlebow.

"It's forgot, Matt," he said. "I'm sorry for any trouble the boy caused y'all, and I'll see to it that it don't happen again. Y'all're welcome at our place anytime."

He reined Button out of the ditch and put him into a canter out the lane toward the Buskin Road. The late March sun softly warmed the morning air.

I'll ride over to Morgan's place this evening and see if he can't bring William over for a turkey hunt one morning next week.

PART III

Chapter Sixteen

October 3, 1906

Almost as tall as Seth, large boned Martha, redheaded and freckled face, walked from the house. She saddled the baby on her hip and shaded his face with her palm raised against the sun and watched Seth and Luke hitch the mules to the wagon. Seth stooped behind the mules and gathered the singletrees and lines, and Luke stood between the mules' heads, gripping the bridle cages.

"Have y'all got in touch with all the folks, Luke?" Martha asked.

"Not yet," Luke said. "I stopped by and told Grandma and Grandpa Knox, and after I helped Grandpa hitch-up, I went to Uncle Morgan and Aunt Amanda's. When I left 'em, they was gathering up to head right on. Then, I stopped and let Doc Foley know Pa was a-needing him again."

"Are you going on over to Aunt Erin and Uncle Richard's place?" Seth said.

"As soon as y'all head out, I'll ride over and tell them," he said.

"You need to go by and tell Matt and Tillie, too, Luke," Seth said.

"I intend to come back home by the cutoff trail and let them know."

"Back 'em up, Luke," Seth said and leaned back, a singletree in either hand, the cotton rope reins draped over his shoulders. "C'mon back, mules. Back, back!"

Luke pushed on the bridle cages, and the mules stepped back.

"Whoa! That's good, Luke," Seth said. He stooped, and the chains clicked and chinked as he hooked the singletrees to the doubletree.

"Come around here and hold Nathan, Luke, while I climb on the wagon," Martha said. Luke stepped to the side of the wagon and took the baby from Martha.

"What're you grinning at, boy?" he said to Nathan and lifted him over his head.

Martha tied the strings of her sunbonnet under her chin.

"Just a minute, Martha," Seth said and wrapped the reins around a seat stanchion. "I'll help you up on the wagon." He took her elbow, and she climbed the wheel spokes onto the seat.

"Alright, Luke," she said. "Hand me up Nathan."

"When you talk to Matt," Seth said. "You could mention to him that some of us might need to spend a night at his place. Maybe a couple nights, depending on how Ma is gittin' on." He climbed onto the seat beside Martha and took up the lines.

"I'll do that." Luke mounted Button and nodded toward the wispy clouds in the southwest sky. "I'd say them horsetail clouds is telling rain."

"Sure enough looks like it," Seth said. "Haw, come up, mules!' He slapped the left line on the lead mule's rump, and the wagon lumbered into motion.

Raising his hand at them, Luke nudged Button's sides with his heels and headed up the Salem Road toward Erin and Richard Hemphill's place.

Seth and Martha had no idea about what had happened at Matt's place, but he knew his ma knew. *Pa would've told her*. And the secret, sad look that he sometimes saw in her eyes when she looked at him, told him that it was so. *Seth and Martha seem to be of a mind that I went back home to give Pa a hand with his ten more acres of cotton*, Luke thought. *I wished to God it was so.*

*

It had been late morning when his pa came back from turkey hunting and had talked to Matt at the turn-row of his cornfield.

"Well, it's taken care of," his pa said.

He halted the mule.

"I just wisht I'd never done it, wisht it never happened." Gripping the plow stock, he looked up at his pa.

"I don't figure he knows or suspects anymore 'n what he saw y'all doing in the kitchen, and Tillie ain't got no call to tell him more. The thing for you to do the first chance you git, is you take him aside and tell him you're regretful about the way you acted with Tillie."

"Pa, I don't know if I can face him or not," he said and turned his head.

"You look at me, Luke. I rode over there not more 'n an hour ago and faced him knowing you was in the wrong, and you had the spit to sit and face him at his supper table for two months while you was laying with his wife."

"Yes sir, but it wa'n't always easy."

"No and facing him now's gonna be harder, but we gotta have peace in this family, and you're the feller that stepped outta the traces and it's hard to plow and step back in 'em at the same time, but you gotta do it." His voice went quiet, and he looked across the new ground toward the house where thin smoke rose from the clay chimney. "Now, buck up, Luke and do what's gotta be done."

And he had been home a little more than a week when Matt and Tillie drove over one morning. They were on their way to visit Tillie's folks and brought Luke the clothes that he'd left at their house. After handshakes and hugs, Thurston said, "Luke, why don't you take Matt out and show him the new cotton field while we brew a pot of coffee?"

"Yes sir, Pa."

At the new ground, Luke stopped and shuffled his feet.

"Matt, I wanna tell you how much I regret acting the way I did with Tillie," he said and looked toward the newly rowed field.

"It's forgot, Luke. We won't ever mention it again." Matt turned and walked back to the house.

Since, they had been cordial with each other at church, but Luke hadn't been back to their house. On the face of it, everything seemed the same as before, but Luke felt a difference in Matt.

And Seth and Martha hadn't even noticed. But to Luke, it was plain. Matt greeted him and talked to him as easily as ever, but he looked at him with eyes flat as stove lids, without depth, like he hid everything that he thought or felt way deep inside.

"I just wisht it'd never happened," he mumbled and tugged the reins to lower Button's head and nudged him with his heels.

*

In the big front room, Retty looked up at the quilt in the quilting frame above her bed and braced herself against the pain that throbbed and flashed up her left leg. If she could just rest easy.

Thurston sat in a straight chair at her bedside.

"I'm of a notion we just pushed too hard to get that new field picked," he said. "I should've sent for Doc Foley the morning you stepped on that thorn," he said, trying to stifle the tremulous fear rising in his throat. The tip of his right forefinger slowly traced the scar that curved from his left fore-knuckle.

On the other side of the room, Thurston's ma and pa sat near the cold fireplace and listened quietly.

Retty turned her head from side to side on the pillow.

"No," she said. As soon as she had brought the eggs in from the henhouse, she had soaked her foot in coal oil, dapped the puncture with turpentine and wrapped the wounded foot in clean cotton ticking. Two days later after the red streak had started up her ankle, Thurston sent Luke for Dr. Foley. He came and said she had done the exact treatment that he would've done.

"Where's Luke, Thurston. I ain't seen him today." She opened her eyes and struggled to relax her clamped jaws.

"He's coming, Retty," he said. "He's gone to fetch Seth and Martha and the baby then he'll be right on. Ma and Pa and Morgan and Amanda and William are already here and Asa and William are playing out back."

"Did Matt come, yet?"

"He'll be along, too, Retty. Maybe tomorrow." She slowly closed her eyes.

Morgan and Amanda returned from the kitchen and shut the door. Morgan sat on a straight chair across the bed from his older brother. Amanda stood behind him, resting one hand on his shoulder. She willed her strength toward Retty, thinking it wasn't much but it was all she had. *Cling to the hem of His coat.*

"Is that Matt?" Retty opened her eyes. "Did Matt come?"

"No, Retty," Thurston said. "It's Morgan and Amanda back from the kitchen."

"Can I get you anything, Retty?" Amanda said.

"No," she said. "Has Ma and Pa Knox left for home yet?"

"Not yet," Morgan said. "They're gonna wait and hear what Dr. Foley has to say."

"Tell 'em they better not wait till after dark to set out," Retty said.

"Don't fret, Retty," Thurston said as he laid a damp cloth across her forehead. "Morgan and Amanda plan to stay over at their place tonight, so they'll have company going home."

"Has Luke come back, yet?" she asked.

"Not yet, but he oughta be along anytime, now," Thurston said. "He's gone to fetch Seth and Martha and the baby to come and see you, and to let Matt and Tillie know."

Fitfully, she turned her head on the pillow.

Poor Matt! To see him suffer pain that I can't succor. Oh, Mavis. If only you were here. Much as I can tolerate. More! But the heart bears all or ceases to beat. Oh, Lord have mercy, spare him! I'll bear all else. Poor, darling Matt! Heart like an angel. So careful and caring of others! My heart broke to hear Thurston tell what happened. Luke and Tillie. Matt like my own child, my oldest son.

She and Thurston had been married about six months when her ma died in childbirth and they closed their house on Buskin Road and moved into the house with her pa and her younger sister, Hannah. She cared for Matt like he was her own baby, her first child. She fed him and rocked him and changed his napkins, and for the first two months of his life, he slept in the same bed with them, and she named him. The next July her pa married, and she and Thurston moved back to their own place where Seth was born that September.

She thought her heart had broken when her ma died, unsmiling, her sad, violet blue eyes marking Retty's heart, and again when her pa died. But those were only sorrows, consolable and even acceptable when considered in the light of God's overall plan of life, death, and redemption.

But what about today's plan? This? Matt deceived? And she saw Mavis smiling at her words with a slow turning of her head. Oh, how she missed Mavis's bright smile and wished she could talk to her for just five minutes, and suddenly, Retty felt ashamed. *Forgive my trespasses. Help my unbelief. God's will be done*.

And Thurston had told her. He came back to bed after starting the fire in the cookstove, and when she rose from bed to fix breakfast, he caught the tail of her nightgown.

"C'mon back to bed, Retty," he whispered. "I wanna tell you something."

"Thurston!" she said. "The young'uns will be up any minute now."

"No," he said. "I need to tell you about Luke coming back home without hat or grip."

She wanted to hear, but suddenly, she was afraid. When he had come back from his morning hunt, she saw him ride out to the new ground and sit on Button and talk to Luke a long while before he came to the house. She wanted to say, "Bear it alone, Thurston," but her throat tightened, and she crawled back into bed. As Thurston told her what had happened in Matt's house and about his talk with Matt, she curled next to him and cried silently, wiping her tears on the pillowcase.

Oh, Matt! A faithless wife conspiring against your trust and with my own blood son! Oh, Lord! How to comfort him when he doesn't even know.

That July, Matt had been elected a deacon in the Mount Olive Baptist Church, and after the service, Tillie caught her aside and told her she was expecting.

"I think he'll come sometimes before Christmas. Maybe in November." Tillie's face shone as she spoke.

Conflicting emotions leapt in Retty's breast as she ciphered months in her head. March, April, May-- February, March, April-- She hugged Tillie and saw Matt just outside the church house door, talking and smiling and shaking hands among a group of men congratulating him on his election as deacon. Tears filled her eyes, and stepping back from Tillie, she opened her purse and took out her handkerchief.

"You're the first one I've told," Tillie whispered. "I ain't had a chance to tell Ma, yet."

"Y'all better ride over there and tell her soon, honey." She dabbed her eyes with the handkerchief and smiled. "I'm so happy for you and Matt. You have told Matt?"

"Oh, yes." Tillie laughed and glanced over her shoulder toward the church house door where Matt smiled and nodded among his well-wishers. "He's about to bust his buttons to tell ever'body."

And she knew what a broken heart felt like.

Help ye my unbelief. God's will be done. And she longed for just ten minutes to talk to Mavis, to have Mavis tell her everything was going to be fine.

At her bedside with elbows on knees, Morgan rested his forehead in his palms and lifted his voice in a prayer that was heard as far as the smokehouse.

Chapter Seventeen

Under the eaves of the smokehouse roof, Asa and William worked to make a blowgun from a five-foot length of switch cane. William butted the smaller end of the cane against a log of the smokehouse and firmly gripped it in both hands. Asa pushed a grater made from a snuff tin lid tacked to the tip of a hickory rod into the larger end and began twisting, reaming the inside of each joint so arrows could be blown smoothly through the blowgun's length.

"Uncle Morgan prays powerful hard," Asa said. He didn't look up from the cane.

"Yeah, since Pa got the call and commenced to preaching over at Shady Grove, it seems like his praying's got more powerful," William said. "Pa says he was mighty sorry that Uncle Thurston went and joined the Baptist. But as powerful as Pa prays, I figure it sets just as good with the Lord for a Baptist as it does for a Methodist."

"He joined the Baptists on account of Ma and all her folks are Baptists," Asa said.

"Well, Grandma and Grandpa Knox is Methodist, too," William said. "Y'all oughta be members over at Shady Grove instead of Mount Olive."

"I wisht we was," Asa said, thinking about Walter Burgess at church down by the spring and he had to be friends with him, now. He had promised his ma.

The Sunday before Luke ran away from home, they'd gone to church like usual, Asa riding up front on the seat next to his pa. Because his ma's back sometimes ached if she rode on the backless wagon seat, she rode on a straight chair in the wagon bed with Callie's chair beside her and Maud and Sarah on chairs behind them. Luke tagged along riding Button. When his pa first rode the horse home, his ma had said, "That little pied horse is purty as a button," and the name stuck. Button hadn't been saddle-broke long, so his pa and Luke rode him a lot just to get him bridlewise. Luke kicked up the horse.

"Pull his head down, son," his pa said. "That's the idee. He's got a smooth trot, but you got to make him keep his head down to put him into gait."

Halfway between home and church, they passed the lane that led to Uncle Matt and Aunt Tillie's place. Uncle Matt was only a year older than Seth, so he and Luke and the older girls called them Matt and Tillie, but Asa and Callie said Uncle Matt and Aunt Tillie. They'd been married about a year. Uncle Matt was his ma's favorite brother. She practically raised him because their ma died when Uncle Matt was a baby, and his ma was always saying how lucky Uncle Matt was to make a catch like Aunt Tillie. That was one of those things that she said, and his pa agreed with like he hadn't even heard what she'd said. Asa thought she was sure enough pretty. She smelled like vanilla flavoring, and a fellow kind of tingled when she smiled at you.

"I guess Matt and Tillie have already left for church," his ma said.

"Yeah," his pa said. "I suspect they'll have a fire built in the heater before Elder Purdy and his folks get there."

"Are you gonna put Matt up for deacon, Thurston?" his ma asked.

"I would. I think him and Tillie's both faithful and dedicated to the church, but I heard Frank Jurgens say he wanted to put Matt's name in consideration, and it might set easier with the other deacons and the congregation, too, somehow, if he did it instead of me, me being his brother-in-law."

When his pa pulled the mules up in front of the church house, Asa climbed out on the front wheel and jumped to the ground.

"Don't you get them clothes dirty, Asa," his ma said.

"No, ma'am. I won't, Ma." He ran down the long slope to the spring at the edge of the woods behind the church house where the boys gathered until time for services to start.

Henry Purdy, Ben Odom, and Walter Burgess, and some more fellows already milled around the spring, laughing and talking. Henry was Elder Purdy's boy. He was fourteen and chewed tobacco. He was always the rooster at the spring, whittling with his Barlow knife and talking about how nice this or that girl's bosoms looked. Henry was careful to talk about girls who went to Shady Grove so as not to offend anybody's women folk that belonged at Mount Olive. He laughed a lot and told story jokes, mostly about Elder Purdy's preaching and sowed them with double handfuls of goddamns and bastards. He said they were alright words because they were in the Bible. He said early on, the Bible told how God damned Adam and Eve, which was where you got goddamn. Further on it said, "No bastard can enter the congregation," which, Henry said, gave us bastard but also showed why they started Methodist churches. Henry declared it was alright to say goddamn and bastard, but all the fellows knew he didn't say those words in front of grown folks.

Next to his cousin William, Ben Odom was Asa's best friend. They sat side by side on the same bench at school and in church, and when their folks visited each other or sat up with sick folks and spent the night, they slept together on a quilt pallet. But they didn't like Walter, even though Maud was sweet on Joe Burgess, Walter's older brother. Walter was big for his age, and he tried to tell jokes like Henry, but his jokes were always mean.

"Looky here," Walter said. "Here comes little Asa Knot-head." Walter glanced at Henry to see if he'd caught his ear, but Henry didn't pay him any mind, never did. "Where'd you get that pink shirt, sonny?"

Asa walked over by Ben and looked up at Walter's ugly blue eyes and hatchet face. Asa and Ben already had talked about how next time Walter picked on them, they weren't going to dare, or double-dog dare, or spit over a stick, but just punch him in the nose and jump on him, fair or not.

"What's the matter, Knot-head?" Walter said. "Cat got your tongue?"

"No." Asa glanced at Ben and grappled to come up with something to say to make Walter look stupid. "I ain't got no cat." He lied.

"I'd venture, you live in a house full of pussies!" Walter snickered and cut his eyes at Henry again. "And you ain't got no cat?" He grabbed a fistful of Asa's shirt, grinning like a mule eating briars through a picket fence. "Looky here, fellers. Asa Knot-head's wearing his sister's pink drawers!" He sniffed the collar. "Pew! Lordy, it is his sister's stinky drawers!"

Asa felt Walter's hot, sour breath on his face, and he trembled, about to cry, which made him madder. His ma did make the shirt from one of Maud's old dresses, but Asa wasn't going to let Walter talk nasty about Maud, even if it wasn't her drawers. He let fly with his fists as hard as he could and lit into him.

Henry and Ben pulled him off Walter. Tears ran down his face, and he brushed them off as fast as he could so nobody would think he was bawling. But Walter bawled without shame, and his nose bled.

"Ain't no fair," Walter said. He held his nose and sobbed, his voice, strange and nasal. "You hit me when I wa'n't looking!"

Some of the fellows laughed and guffawed, and Walter set out for the church house, still holding his nose. Asa heaved a deep sigh, his breath catching and jerking in his chest, and wiped his sleeve across his face and spat.

"Way to go, Asa." Ben patted his back.

"You showed him, boy," somebody said from across the spring.

"About goddamn time one o' you boys licked that little bastard's ass," Henry said. Casually, he spat a gob of tobacco juice and shaved another curl from his whittling stick.

Ben dipped a gourd dipper into the spring and handed it to Asa. He drank, and though his hands shook, he grinned. He had licked Walter Burgess.

"I'm obliged, Ben," Asa said. He drank and handed the empty dipper back to Ben.

"Good goddamn," Henry said. "Here comes Brother Thurston, and you can bet them goddamn Indian eyes is blazing like a lightered pine knot." Keeping his head down like he was busy whittling, Henry edged to the other side of the spring and sort of stood among the other fellows.

Asa looked up the slope toward the church house, and sure enough, it was his pa. He could tell by the frown on his face and the way his mustache jutted over his clamped lips that he was fit to be tied. Without breaking stride, he cut a switch from a low branch of the first beech tree he came to and trimmed it as he walked. Folding his knife, he dropped it into his pocket. Asa's heart thumped like a snared rabbit's, and all the fellows stepped back from him but Ben, and Ben patted Asa on the back again.

"C'mon, boy," his pa said. He didn't even look at Henry or Ben or any of the other fellows around the spring. He took hold of Asa's wrist with one hand and swatting the beech switch on his own britches leg, he led Asa back up the slope toward the church house.

"Boy," he said. "You may not learn nothing else at church, but you're gonna learn to act like a gentleman and not some kinda heathen."

"He started it, Pa," Asa said. He sobbed, but he couldn't help it. "He said--"

"I don't care what he said or did. I'm not gonna whip you on account of what he said. Look at them clothes. Your ma sews and washes and scrubs and irons trying to keep you looking fitting and you go getting in fights and wallowing in the dirt at church like some kinda ruffian."

At the front of the church house, several young fellows, along with Luke and Joe Burgess, Walter's older brother, milled around the churchyard lost as a durn bunch of dry cows at milking time. They talked and shuffled their feet while they finished their smokes or chews before going in for church, except Luke didn't chew or smoke.

His pa stopped at the foot of the steps, held Asa by the arm, and switched his legs. He did a dance right there in front of all those older fellows, but not one of them dared to smile or even act like they saw what was happening.

"Now, you get in there and set with your ma and don't let me hear no more outta you, young man," his pa said.

"Yes sir." Whimpering, Asa climbed the steps, and his pa snapped the switch in two and tossed it aside.

"And y'all could keep a closer eye on them young'uns, Luke," his pa said.

"Yes sir, Pa," Luke said.

His pa herded him through the door and right down the aisle. Asa saw Walter sitting with his ma and pa. He held a handkerchief under his nose and ignored Asa's stare. Walter was a coward, and even though he sat right in the middle of the church, Asa figured he was a bastard like Henry said and would be kicked out of the congregation as soon as the grown folks found it out. He wished he'd punched him in the nose at school last summer, now.

At the front row, his pa put Asa between his ma and Sarah, and he went and sat on the bench beside the pulpit with the other deacons. Asa snuffled, and his ma gave him her handkerchief. He wiped his nose, and every now and then sneaked a look at the deacons' bench, but his pa kept his head bowed most of the time.

They sang a few hymns, and then Elder Purdy set in to preaching about what a fearful thing it was to fall into the hands of the living God. His voice went up and down, and directly, he looked at the deacons, and his pa or Mr. Jurgens or one of the others shouted, "A-men!" Asa figured that must be why his pa kept his head bowed most of the time, so's he could shout, "A-men!" when he took a notion to and not when Elder Purdy gave him a sign to.

Elder Purdy finally tuckered out and called on his pa to pray. His pa slid from the end of the deacons' bench and hit the floor on one knee and propped his elbow on his thigh, and resting his forehead in his hand, he commenced to pray.

*

The ride home rolled in quiet agony for Asa. He sat as far from his pa as he could without falling off the seat. His ma and pa talked about Elder Purdy's sermon and how Sister Purdy was such a help to him and how well behaved their young'uns were. They always seemed to talk about how well-behaved other young'uns were after he'd got a whipping. Neither said anything about his getting into a fight, but anytime their talk slowed or took a new turn, he hunched his shoulders, afraid his name was about to come up.

Luke rode along on Asa's side of the wagon. He knew Luke wanted him to look at him so he could smile like everything was alright, but Asa kept his eyes straight ahead. Up the road, Uncle Matt stood at the turnoff lane, while Aunt Tillie waited on their wagon.

"Whoa, mules," his pa said. "Y'all have a breakdown, Matt?"

"No. Nothing such as that, Thurston," Uncle Matt said. He held his hat in his hand. "I know it ain't my place to say it, but don't you think you was a mite hard on Asa? I suspect Walter Burgess was the feller that oughta got what Asa got." As he spoke, Uncle Matt nodded toward Asa, and Asa turned his head, afraid his pa was going to look at him.

Durn, Uncle Matt!

Asa shifted his eyes through the woods until he caught sight of a yaupon bush, green and speckled with red berries and brighter in the winter sunshine than it really was and hunching his shoulders making himself as small as he could, he stared at the bush.

"I thank you for your words and your concern, Brother Matt," his pa said. "But if you'll see after your household, I'll see after mine." He slapped the cotton plow line along the lead mule's back. "Gee! Come up, mules."

*

At the sound of thumping hooves, Asa looked up from the blowgun and saw a man on a gray horse riding up the Buskin Road from the south. The rider sat upright, almost stiff in the saddle. He firmly gripped the reins in his left hand, and his right arm dropped straight from his shoulder along his side. A wide brim straw hat slanted across his face that was covered by a full gray beard. His duster, linen coat and vest gaped open under the savage October sun revealing a red shirt with ruffles down the front.

"Here comes Doc Foley now," Asa said, and William loosened his grip on the blowgun and peered round the corner of the smokehouse.

An old man, Asa thought, and raised the cane to his mouth and blew a puff of powdered scrapings from the tube. *Old as Grandpa Knox. Grandma says he was in the War. Rode with Grandpa and Uncle Jim and Uncle Dave Knox. Killed more 'n he's healed. Grandma says*.

"Has he got his pill bag?" William said.

"Yeah, it's hanging on his saddle horn," Asa whispered as Dr. Foley neared the side gate.

Heart like a needle, Grandma says. Fine doctor, though. Grandma…

"How do, boys."

"Howdy, Dr. Foley," Asa said, and William nodded.

They edged from the corner of the smokehouse to near the gate and watched as the old doctor slowly stepped from the saddle and looped the bridle reins round a fence picket. He peeled off his duster, laid it across the saddle, and lifted his battered, black leather satchel from the saddle pommel.

"Looks like y'all 'bout got a blowgun made," he said. He lifted the gate latch and stepped into the yard. *A fellow can't tell one of these Knox young'uns from another. Like a flock of Dominicker chickens, these young Knoxs.*

"Yes sir," Asa said. "Luke burnt the joints outta this one for us." He held out the cane for Dr. Foley to see. *Did Luke ride right up to his front gate? Or whistle? Or did he ride up the lane waving a white handkerchief like Grandma says Uncle Dave did after him and Grandpa had a fistfight? Fisticuffs for an hour, Grandma says.*

"You boys better wait 'til after the first frost before y'all go to killing any rabbits," Dr. Foley said. "They'll still be wormy and apt to give you rabbit fever."

"Yes sir," Asa said. "That's what Grandma Knox said, too."

"Aunt Retty's down sick," William said.

Dr. Foley nodded. *Morgan's boy. A hard birthing this lad. No more birth pangs for his ma.*

"Well, Retty Knox is a mighty tough lady, and we're gonna see if we can't get her back up on her feet." He laid his free hand on Asa's head and gently shook it.

“Grandma and Grandpa’s done here, and Ma and Pa’s in there with’em,” William said.

“I thought I recognized Brother Morgan’s praying when I rode up,” Dr. Foley said. “I’d better get on in there and see if I can’t give him a hand.” He smiled down at the boys and jutted his lower lip and shaking his head, he turned and walked toward the house.

Dominicker chickens, these Knox young ‘uns.

He climbed the steps onto the back porch. His worn satchel hanging from his left hand bumped his leg at each step. Pausing on the threshold of the open door, he doffed his hat, scraped his shoe soles and peered into the shade of the quiet room.

Amanda stood behind Morgan, her hand resting on his shoulder. At the sound of his shoes scraping on the porch, she looked and saw Dr. Foley. The hem of her dress whispered just above the plank floor as she hurried to him and extended her hand.

“C’mon in, Dr. Foley,” she said. “We’re mighty pleased to see you. Let me take your hat.”

“I’m obliged, Sister Amanda,” he said. *Do what I can. All I can do*. And as always, he felt a twinge of discomfort on hearing the faith folks placed in his reputation as a healer. Twenty years ago, some folks had lived through a siege of swamp fever after he had sat at their bedsides. All he was able to do was take their temperature and wipe their faces with a damp cloth and wrap them in wet flannel to keep their fever down. Those and the families of those who lived through the siege reckoned him a healer, and the families of those who’d died reckoned their loved ones had been beyond human help. Since, he had plodded from sickbed to household, dragging the misplaced faith of his patients like a shaggy beast of burden.

He had apprenticed his trade as a surgical orderly, wielding bone saw and scalpel from Choctaw Bayou through the Red River Campaign, and later, after the War, he and his brothers pooled their finances, and he returned to his studies in New Orleans, and earned papers that officially declared him a competent practitioner of medicine. But despite his reputation and official papers, Sam Foley knew that ultimately everybody was beyond human help, that all he could do, all any physician could do, was to try and give comfort to the sick and dying.

He handed Amanda his weathered hat and smiled and nodded at Grandma Knox seated near the hearth. *Old Dominicker hen, herself.*

"How do, Onie?" he said.

"Tolerable well, Sam." Onie returned his nod, her eyes dark and shining. "And yourself?"

"Better'n an old man's expectations oughta be."

"Sam," George Knox said and pushed up from his chair. They shook hands.

"You're looking fit to dress, George," Dr. Foley said.

"I got my complaints, Sam," George said and tugged his small white goatee.

"I'm gonna move to the front porch and take some fresh air," Onie said. She rocked forward out of her chair and stood up with effort. Clutching her Bible to her bosom in one hand, she smoothed the skirts of her gabardine dress with the other. "You coming with me, Pa?"

"Naw, I'm gonna get them boys out there to help me see to Sam's horse," George said. "Morgan, why don't you and Amanda make a fresh pot of coffee?"

"That's a good idee, Pa," Morgan said.

"That was a mighty powerful prayer you made, Brother Morgan," Dr. Foley said.

"I'm obliged that you say so, Dr. Foley. But give God all the glory."

"I always do, Brother Morgan. I always do."

In the light shuffle of feet and the rustle of skirts, they left the room. Thurston rose and shook hands with the doctor.

"You take this chair, Dr. Foley," he said. "I'm a-needing to stand and stretch my joints a bit."

"Thank you, Thurston," Dr. Foley said. He eased himself onto the hard seat of the straight chair, set his medical bag on the floor next to him, opened it, and pulled out his stethoscope. He hung it from his neck and let it dangle like a charm. For a long moment, he watched Retty's chest rise and fall with rapid, shallow breathing.

"Bear with me, Retty," he said, and taking his spectacles from his shirt pocket, he hooked the legs behind his ears. "I'm gonna examine you, but if I hurt you, let me know."

She nodded.

Dr. Foley rose from the chair, bent over, and peered into her eyes.

"Look up, Retty. Down. Left. Right."

Sitting down, he plugged the stethoscope into his ears. He leaned forward pressed the cone to her chest and jutted his lower lip.

"Take a deep breath, Retty. Let 'er go." He moved the cone from place to place on her chest and torso. "Again." He nodded and grunted.

Faster heartbeat. He sat back in the chair. *No skip, yet*.

Turning his large, gray head from one side to the other, he unhooked the stethoscope from his ears and let it hang from his neck.

"I'm gonna have a look at that foot now, Retty." He lifted the quilt and looked for a long moment. *Make comfortable if I can. All I can do if I can.*

He pulled the quilt over her legs and reached the thermometer from his shirt pocket.

Chapter Eighteen

Onie settled into a rocking chair near the edge of the front porch where she could safely skite her snuff into the yard. She rested her small, parchment-colored hands on the worn cover of the Bible in her lap and frowned against the brute afternoon sun and gazed at Thurston's cotton field that had been picked over once. More cotton had opened since the first picking and drooled from gaping burs.

Slowly, she fished a snuff tin wrapped in a cambric handkerchief from her dress pocket. With ritual deliberation, she spread the handkerchief over her Bible and twisted the lid from the snuff tin. She pinched her lower lip between her thumb and forefinger of one hand, tilted the snuff tin over the pocket of her pinched lip and tapped the side of the tin with her finger. The pungent tobacco smell commingled with that of biscuits, bacon and woodsmoke. She pushed the lid on the snuff can and slipped it into her pocket and laid a hand at her throat. Her fingers touched a necklace of fine, opaque red, yellow, and blue beads, and she thought, *Oh, Retty*. And she began to pray, *Jesus Christ, son of God, have mercy on a sinner like me*.

She prayed differently from most folks. Her prayer poured out, overflowing, a prayer from her spirit and by her spirit, and not from her mind and not a prayer of hopelessness or despair or supplication but of thanksgiving and acceptance. Beginning in words, she continued without words, or if there were words, she wasn't aware of forming or understanding them. Her praying was a heavy groaning. And since the summer she lived with her grandma and grandpa Thurston, she had known that she was different.

*

Dr. Foley pulled the thermometer from Retty's mouth. Pinching it in his fingers, he held it up to catch the light, and with a pensive backward tilt of the head, he squinted through his spectacles at the mercury column.

“Has she got a temperature?” Thurston asked from the foot of the bed.

“Looks like a hundred and a couple o’ tenths, maybe.” Dr. Foley glanced up at Thurston and shook the thermometer with several snaps of his wrist and slipped it into his shirt pocket. “That’s not much fever.”

“What d’you think, Doc? How’s she doing?”

“It appears like the poison is still spreading, but she’s strong, and with some rest, she has a chance to fight it off. I’ll be coming back over in the morning,” he said, thinking that if she was still alive, there’d be hope for one more day.

For a moment, he sat pensively and didn’t look at Thurston. Unhooking the stethoscope from his neck, he carefully folded the tubes and stuffed it into his satchel then rummaged the inside pockets of the medicine bag until he found a bottle of reddish-brown liquid.

“She’ll be up and around in a day or two,” Thurston said.

Grunting and nodding his head, Dr. Foley stood. Years of practice had taught him that a combination of patience, acquiescence and compassion was the surest way to deal with hopeless hope. *Don’t break hope*. He knew death when he sat in its presence. *Listeth like the wind. But don’t break hope; hope fades to hope, sure and steadfast, soon enough.*

“We’ll be keeping an eye on her,” Dr. Foley said and handed him the bottle. “Give her eight or twelve drops of this in a half a drinking glass of water every three or four hours. It’ll help to ease her.”

“Should I mix her some now?” he said. He closed his hand around the bottle and looked at the clock on the mantelpiece.

“Yes sir,” Dr. Foley said. “I figure if she ain’t been easy in two days and nights, she’s needing rest.”

"Is that potion gonna put me to sleep, Dr. Foley?"

"I hope it does, Retty," he said. He took off his spectacles, folded them, and pushed them into the same shirt pocket with his thermometer. "You're about burnt out from fighting pain, and that laudanum will ease you sure."

"Not yet," she said. "I wanna see Nathan and talk to Seth and Luke and the girls before you dose me up."

"I can't fault you there, Retty. Y'all got a mighty fine-looking grandson and healthy as a horse."

"Can it wait awhile?" Thurston asked.

"I wouldn't put it off more than a half-hour, an hour at the most," he said. "She's needing relief and rest."

"I'll see to it Doc," he said. "Now, you take a seat in the rocker over there by the window and I'll fetch Pa. I know y'all wanna visit while you're having your coffee."

He left the room with the bottle, and Dr. Foley patted Retty's hand and shuffled across the room. He set his bag on the floor next to the fireplace and lowered himself into the rocking chair. Glancing over his shoulder through the window at his back, he watched Onie rocking back and forth.

Old Dominecker hen. He smiled to himself. He looked around and brushed the lower edge of his mustache with the knuckle of his forefinger as Thurston followed George through the back door and sat at Retty's bedside. He watched his old comrade as he walked across the room. *George is getting old. How old? Sixty-three, -four*?

"Keep your seat. Sam," George said. His words were a manner of greeting. Sam hadn't attempted to rise.

"How're you feeling these days, George?" George was a couple of years younger than Sam, and Sam remembered with a start that he was sixty-eight years old.

"I've got my complaints," George said, and sat in an armchair on the opposite side of the fireplace.

"That old arm ain't bothering you again, is it?"

"Naw, naw," George said, and pursing his lips, he tugged his chin whiskers. "My arm's tolerable, but it's got to where I can't sleep the night through."

"Ghosts ain't haunting you, are they?" Sam glanced out the window again and saw Onie's gray head arc to and fro as she slowly rocked. He smiled.

"Shah. I'll venture, my dang bladder's shrunk."

"Yeah," Sam said. "It's a medical fact that ever'thing shrinks in old age but your nose and your feet. Worst part is there's no remedy for it known to man."

Amanda walked into the room carrying a blue patterned cup in a matching saucer.

"Here's your coffee, Dr. Foley,"

"Thank you, honey." He leaned forward and took the china from her hand, and she walked to Retty's bedside and sat on the chair across the bed from Thurston.

"You gonna drink with me, George?"

"You go ahead, Sam," George said. "I only drank it in the mornings. My dang bladder won't handle it."

"I oughta quit it myself," Sam said. "But it does help get me through the day."

Sam poured the black, steaming coffee into the saucer, blew on it, and slurped. Savoring the bitter draught, he peered over the saucer into George Knox's cold, blue eyes. George was one of seven on the jury. He and George and George's two older brothers, Jim and Dave Knox and Henry Jurgens, Hugh Odom, and Brother Cicero Inglish composed the jury. Jim Knox was captain. Twelve all told in the company. Twenty-three in their company before they were able to drive the Jayhawkers from the parish. Quorum of seven, then. Strange, hard days. Cold night. Barn cold night. December cold. Seven counting George and him. Thirty years ago, thirty-five? Strange, hard times.

Chapter Nineteen

The men's voices cut the cold odor of musty hay and dust as they argued under the glow of a lantern in Henry Jurgens's barn. Sam had delivered Jim's call to assemble, mouth to ear, to five other members of the company. Tom Jenkins, whose loyalty was in question, wasn't among those he summoned.

"I don't like it one dang bit, Jim," Henry Jurgens said. "If a man's gonna be accused of something, he oughta be here to answer for hisself." Henry was always contrary and argumentative. Before the fight at the Mounds, Colonel Ramsey said he would've had Henry's mule-headed arse shot but he was the best scout in the battalion, and in any case, Henry was in the right.

"You wa'n't at the meeting in September when Tom accused you," Dave Knox said. He leveled his quiet voice at Henry.

"What d'you mean, accused me?" Henry's eyes narrowed. "Accused me of what?"

"Of being a spy, Henry," Sam said. "Of being a traitor, of taking money from Caleb Wicker. Tom said you sold Fergus Littleberry to Wicker and the Jayhawkers which would mean you also sold Arnold Spriggs."

"That's a lie!" Henry said. "I ain't never said more 'n two words to that Jayhawker bastard."

"We know that for a certainty now, Henry," Jim Knox said. "But we had to find out who did sell Fergus. The Jayhawkers burned him out and killed or stole all his stock, and as long as we've got a spy amongst us, ain't none of us gonna be safe."

"How do y'all know it's Tom Jenkins? Maybe it is me. Maybe it's Sam or Hugh or you, Jim."

"Who're you accusing, Henry?" Dave Knox asked.

"Why, I ain't accusing nobody, Dave." Henry swallowed and quickly looked at Jim.

"Then shut your gob and..."

"Here. Dave," Jim said. "Ever'body stand easy, and I'll give y'all the case and the facts."

Henry Jurgens nodded and lowered his eyes, and Dave Knox faded into the dim, outer edge of the lantern light.

"In early September we all know that Fergus Littleberry's place was ransacked and burned and that him and his folks was lucky to get away alive. Word was sent to all five commanders of the companies in Okaloosa Parish that there was a spy among us and to keep a sharp lookout. Later that month, we met on the Hennessey Creek below Hugh's place and ever'body here was at that meeting and so was Tom Jenkins, and I told y'all a Judas was amongst us. About a week later, Tom come to me and said he suspicioned Henry of being the Judas, so I called a meeting of ever'body but you, Henry, and Tom accused you to us, giving two different times and places that you met with Caleb Wicker."

"That's a damn lie!"

"Stand easy, Henry," Jim said. "It was hard for any of us to believe that anybody in our company was a traitor, but then and there, I detailed Tom to keep an eye on you, to see where you went and who you talked to and to report to me and nobody else, and we broke up the meeting.

"The next day, I rode over to Sam's place and detailed him to watch Tom. I figured Sam, being a doctor, could ride all over the countryside day or night, without raising suspicions, and I told him not to say anything about watching Tom to anybody but me."

"I don't like all this slippin' round and spyin' in the dark like a nest of rats," Henry said.

"Nobody here does," Sam said. "But so long as these Jayhawkers are running roughshod over us, decent folks won't be allowed to vote or serve on juries, unless you wanna join these radical Republicans and then all you'll have to vote for are scallywags and carpetbaggers, and we're gonna have judges like Douglas Cranford and a sheriff like Caleb Wicker. Cranford is a carpetbagger from Ioway or Kansas or God knows where and Wicker is a scalawag from Alexandria. Both are pocket change to the Jayhawkers. They're all rats, Jayhawkers and all, and we're gonna have to fight 'em like the rats they are until we run 'em outta the country."

"Stand easy," Jim said. "Now, after I talked to Sam, I rode over and told Brother Cicero that I'd rethought it and decided one man couldn't keep an eye on Henry by hisself, so me and him and my brother, George, oughta take turns watching Henry, too, but we should keep it quiet because I didn't want word to get back to Tom and for him to think I didn't trust him. Make him feel like I was slighting him."

Jim paused and looked from face to face round the circle.

"That's the case," Jim said. "But I wanna say one more thing before I give the facts and evidence. We all fought with Colonel Isacc Ramsey except for Brother Inglish here, and he fought in the Washington Avengers. When I heard there was a traitor in one of the Okaloosa Parish companies, I couldn't think of a man-jack among our company that it could be. Then, when Tom accused Henry, I suspicioned the Judas was amongst us, and he was either Henry or Tom. That's how come I set up the spy ring the way I did.

"Now, Tom has been passing tales on to me for two, almost three months. He told me the times Henry rode to Clemson and met with Wicker and--"

"I ain't left my place but to--"

"Shut up, Henry!" Jim said. "I know where you been to and what you been doing. Damn, Colonel Ike was right, and he oughta have had you shot for arguing with an officer and said he would've if you hadn't been in the right."

The men chortled and elbowed each other, nodding their heads.

"Alright, men, stand easy, and let's get done here." Jim looked around the group and shook his head. "Now, Tom told me times and places Henry met Wicker on the road between his place and Clemson. All this time, me and Brother Cicero or George was watching Henry too, and he ain't left his place but to haul corn to grind over to Rufe Tarroll's grist mill or to visit folks here in the community or to go to church, and me or Brother Cicero or George was with him or watching him ever trip he made. So, we know Tom Jenkins is lying about what Henry did, but why? Well, Sam was keeping an eye on Tom and ever'time Tom said Henry met Wicker, Sam saw Tom heading for Clemson. Three weeks ago this past Saturday, Sam followed Tom to Clemson and went to a coupla stores like he had business, and saw Tom go into the sheriff's office. Now, what's Tom Jenkins doing in the sheriff's office if he's not there to see Caleb Wicker? Pass on information and collect his pay? And this is the worst part, the day Sam saw Tom going to see Wicker was two days before the Jayhawkers burned Arnold Spriggs out and killed his oldest boy. That's the case, facts and evidence. Anybody wanna say anything?"

"Yeah, I do," Brother Inglish said. "We know for certain that Henry here hasn't been talking to Wicker, and we know that Tom's been lying about Henry, but if Tom's the Judas, why haven't any of us been burned out?"

"I had the same question," Jim said. "And I talked it over with Sam, and he come up with what I figure is the right answer. Tell 'em what your idee is, Sam."

"First thing, men, is you can bet your boots that Caleb Wicker's got most of our names if not all our names," Sam said and looked at Brother Inglish, then at Henry. "But he's saving us for last. If we were the only ones getting burnt out and killed that would make it plain to us and the other companies that the traitor was in our company, but if the Jayhawkers burnt out one man at a time in different companies, it'd scare hell outta all of us, and we would have no idee who it is or what company he's in, and we'd set in to distrusting one another and ever'body. That way, the Jayhawkers would break us up before we can break them up."

"Anybody else wanna talk?" Jim said.

"Yeah, Jim. Sam says he figures Wicker has our names," Hugh Odom said. "What're we gonna do about that?"

"We'll deal with Wicker when the time comes," Jim said. "Sam is out and about on his sick calls and visits with his ears to the ground. He'll know when the time comes to deal with Wicker."

"Put it to the vote, Jim," Brother Inglish said softly.

"Is ever'body ready to vote on a verdict?" Jim said.

Heads nodded around the circle.

"Brother Cicero, guilty or not guilty?" Jim said.

"Guilty."

"George?"

"Guilty as hell!"

"Henry?"

"Twice guilty!"

When the polling was finished, all seven had voted guilty, and Jim took off his hat.

"Ever'body unnerstood when we took the oath that the penalty for treason is death," he said. "Now we have to choose, by lots, the one to do the deed."

"Ain't no need in that, Jim," Dave Knox said. "You fellers just go on home and count the deed done."

"You know we can't do it that way, Dave," Jim said. "It has to be done by lots so nobody will know who done the deed but the man hisself, and God." He stepped closer to the lantern and opened his hand in the dim light.

"I want y'all to gather up and count the beans in my hand."

Six red beans and one white bean lay in his palm.

"The man who draws the white bean does the deed." Jim poured the beans into his hat, shook it, and walked away from the lantern. "Y'all want me to draw first or last?"

"Go ahead," Sam said.

"Yes, Jim. Have done with yours," Brother Inglish said.

Jim raised the hat above his head, reached in, pinched up a bean and curled it into his fist. He went to the lantern, and with his back to the others so none could see, he opened his hand and looked at the bean. He put it into his coat pocket and returned to the group, all the while holding the hat above his head.

"I'll draw next," Sam said and reached into the hat and went to the lantern. The others waited, shuffling their feet, vaguely murmuring about the cold weather then followed in turn. Each reached into Jim's hat, and stepping under the lantern light, read his fate in secret, slipped it into his pocket and returned to the group.

"That's done," Jim said. "Do the deed soon. Do it in secret and leave the white bean for a sign. It'll scare hell outta them Jayhawkers to find one of their dead toadies with a sure sign on him."

No one ever knew for a certainty which man drew the white bean. The deed was done, but there wasn't a white bean anywhere on or near Tom Jenkins's body. Sam thought it possible that someone with a personal grudge had killed him. No one would've known for certain who did it, yet, if Dave Knox had lived. Onie Knox told it, then, after Dave was killed.

*

"You headed back to your place when you leave here, Sam?" George said, breaking the silence.

Cold, blue eyes, Sam thought, and said, "Yeah, I've got to do all my milking and feeding and cooking, too, since I lost Claudia." He set his cup on the saucer, and balancing the china in one hand, brushed the knuckle of his forefinger along the under edge of his mustache.

"Lordy." George said and glanced at Thurston sitting quietly at Retty's bedside. "That's gotta be hard on a man in his old age."

"It is for a fact, George," he said, thinking, Dave's eyes were blue-gray. Like a clean knife blade.

"Me and Onie need to get on home and feed and milk before dark, too, and we're gonna take Asa and William home with us for the night," George said. "It looks like it's gonna cloud up and rain, too."

"Maybe hail," Sam said, jutting his lower lip and nodding his head. *Jim had cold blue eyes, like George*.

"That'd be about the luck of it," George said. "Thurston's got maybe four or five bales of cotton in a second picking still in the field."

"Yeah, just when you figure on a good year, it sets in to raining come pickin' time," he said and thought, *or your wife ups and dies on you*. "There ain't no human help for it, and sometimes, I'm of a mind the Good Lord Himself don't give a hang one way or the other." He wondered if his eyes told that they were the last thing that Caleb Wicker ever saw in this world.

"You finish your coffee, Sam." George pushed himself from his chair by the armrest. "I'm gonna go get them boys to help me hitch-up, and we'll ride along with you as far as our place."

"Mighty fine, George," Sam said and looked over his shoulder. *There ain't no human help for it.* With steady hands, he poured the last of his coffee into the saucer, slowly raised it to his lips, and blew wrinkles across the bitter draught. *Old Dominecker hen. She knows things she don't see and don't know some things that she does see.*

Chapter Twenty

The summer she lived with her grandma and grandpa Thurston, Onie was five years old, and her ma and pa had just got married. The man her ma married was not her pa, but she always loved him and called him Pa. His last name was Morgan, and hers was Thurston, just like grandma and grandpa's and her ma's name before she got married. She didn't know her pa's name. She'd heard grown folks talking when they didn't know she was about and listening or maybe they knew she was listening and didn't care that she overheard them. They said things that she knew were about her and her pa or her not having a pa like other young'uns. They said words she didn't understand, but she remembered the words and later understood them. They said such things as, "I'd venture to say, you can't tell for a certainty who sired a woods colt," or "Like a feller says, you never know where a woods colt's blood runs," and seeing her, inclined their heads with sly smiles. And the disembodied words lingered in her memory, but she could make no sense of them drifting in the darkness. She became uneasy in the presence of some grown folks, grown folks with sly smiles. As she grew older, slowly at first then suddenly, the overheard words took form and meaning just as form and meaning came to her through shadow and darkness as she and her ma walked from home to Grandma Thurston's house just at daybreak one June morning. She saw an old man, hatless with a pipe clamped in his mouth hunched motionless atop the road bank in the next curve. She almost froze in mid-step. He didn't move. Her ma didn't seem to take notice of him. Maybe he didn't see them. She smelled tobacco smoke, and her scalp tightened and prickled. As the light increased and they drew nearer, the old man suddenly became a storm-broke stump, clear and distinct against the woods. And in the same gradual, sudden way, the words of the grown folks she had overheard became clear and distinct through the haze of years when she thought about what they had said and about the old woman who came to see her the summer her ma and pa got married.

That summer she lived with Grandma and Grandpa Thurston almost until picking time. Sometimes cousins visited and played with her, but usually, she built her stick houses and tended her corncob and chicken feather dolls alone in the sand of the front yard. A picket fence around the yard kept cows from browsing Grandma's rose bushes and hogs from wallowing in the cool dust under the house. The afternoon the old woman came, Grandpa Thurston idled in the shade on the porch and smoked his pipe while she sat in the sand and carefully stacked sticks raising a new barn on her place.

"What're you doing here at my house, Mary Tupper?" Grandpa said. His voice startled Onie from her barn-raising.

She looked up, unsure if he had spoken to her. He rose from his chair and walked to the near edge of the porch.

"I come to see the child."

Onie looked up toward the sound of the strange voice, her hand shading her eyes from the bald sun in a clear sky, high and bright. The old woman stood outside the picket fence, her face, round and flat, and her coarse white hair, streaked with black, was rolled in a ball on top of her head. The frayed hem of her gingham dress brushed the ground, and her bare brown feet splayed like a duck's feet.

"Where's your old man at?" Grandpa said. "Where's Abraham?"

"He's a-waitin' for me down by the sycamore tree," she said.

"It's a far piece from Nashobee Lake, Mary Tupper."

"It's a longer walk."

"A mighty long walk to where you ain't askt nor wanted and ain't got no business a-bein' at in the first place." Grandpa pointed his pipe stem at her like a pistol.

"I brought gifts for the child," she said. "I brought her two gifts."

"I recollect that we agreed there'd be none of this."

"Maybe y'all agreed to that."

"You're an Indian Giver, Mary Tupper."

"Aye, Jacob Thurston. I gave my grandchild and my son."

"There'll be none of that, neither!" Grandpa said, his voice shrill, and his face reddened, and his hand trembled as he pushed his smoking pipe into his pants pocket. "His name's not to pass between us. You do recollect that, don't you, Mary Tupper?"

"Aye, I recollect that. But I came to bring gifts to the child, not to say his name."

"Well, what did you bring her?" Grandpa said, his voice relenting.

"I brought her this book" she said and raised a Bible in her hand. "And some neck-beads."

"Huh. What did you write in that Bible, Mary Tupper?"

"I wrote nothing," she said. "I can't write."

"Who wrote in it for you?"

"Only the God, as far as I can tell."

"Alright, Onie," Grandpa said. "Get what Mary Tupper brought you and bring it here. I wanna see what it is."

Her hands behind her back, sliding her bare feet in the hot sand, Onie sidled to the fence. The old woman smiled, and her eyes, dark as chinquapins, lighted in her wizened face.

"Take this book, child."

She took the Bible, and the old woman leaned over the pickets and hovering over Onie, she tied a necklace of beads around her neck. Onie smelled woodsmoke, bacon grease, and a faint dusting of snuff, and saw a necklace of the same colors and pattern around the old woman's neck.

"Bring that Bible here to me, Onie," Grandpa said. Walking down the porch steps, he pulled his spectacles from his shirt pocket and set them on his nose and hooked the legs behind his ears. He took the

Bible from her and glanced at the beads around her neck. He gave a humorless snort and opened the Bible. He thumbed through the pages, then closed it and folded his spectacles.

"I guess she can keep 'em, Mary Tupper."

"Aye."

"But y'all're gonna have to agree that none of y'all will ever come up here to see her again, or nowheres else to see her."

"Aye," she said. "I agree."

"And your old man? Abraham? Does he agree, too?" He raised the Bible in one hand, striking the bargain with a threat.

"He agrees, too," she said.

"This child ain't never gonna hear his name," Grandpa said. He handed Onie the Bible, pulled the pipe from his pocket, and stuck the bit into his mouth.

"No," Mary Tupper said. She looked into Onie's eyes, and a smile touched her lips as her fingertips read the beads at her throat. "Never."

Onie remembered Mary Tupper's words and how they were said, and the old, dusky woman anxiously tarrying while Grandpa Thurston thumbed through the Bible and how she felt different; estranged and apart, as much on the outside as the old woman who stood on the other side of the fence clutching the pickets. She had been sought and found, and even though a child, she remembered yet the unspoken, the unspeakable, which had passed between them.

*

The bright, October sun tinged the air with a brassy haze. A redbird landed in the green foliage of a wax myrtle shrub just inside the front gate and ruffled its feathers.

Onie stretched over the rocking chair arm toward the end of the porch and braced her lips with forked fingers and spat. Several brown and yellow hens waddled across the yard. Clacking loudly, they flapped their wings and hopped about, greedily sparring for the wet globules of dust. Onie settled back into the chair, wiped her handkerchief across her mouth, and again deliberately spread the linen over her Bible.

The old woman's fingertips read her neck-beads, and she continued to pray from her spirit, an awful acceptance groaning in her breast.

The front door opened, and a flurry burst from the wax myrtle shrub, and the redbird fled over the cotton field toward the distant line of trees.

"Ma," George said, leaning out the door. "I got the wagon all hitched up. You better tell Thurston and Retty your good-byes. We need to get them young'uns and ourselves to the house before it sets in to raining."

Chapter Twenty-one

Tillie sat on the front porch and hummed. The faint odor of clean earth rose from the dishpan of Irish potatoes she was peeling for supper. Occasionally, she glanced up to watch Matt picking cotton in the field across the lane. Her cheeks blushed in the October heat of early afternoon.

Looking to her left beyond the barn, she saw Luke riding his paint horse up the cutoff trail. Her hands paused. Carefully she laid her paring knife in the dishpan, set it on the seat of the chair next to her, and leaning forward, hands on knees, she rose. Slowly brushing her skirts straight, she walked to the edge of the porch.

Matt saw him too and walked from the field and dropped a nearly filled cotton sack over the rail fence then climbed over and waited beside the lane. Luke pulled Button to a stop and stepped down from the saddle. He and Matt shook hands.

She heard their voices but couldn't understand their words. Their faces appeared serious, even grave. Matt stood with his hands on his hips and shifted his weight to one leg, and Luke stood in front of him and slapped the ends of the bridle reins across his open palm as they talked. She wondered now that she had let it go as far as she did, knowing it was foolishness from the outset. It would be easy enough to say she couldn't help herself, but she knew she could have and did when the time came. *Thank God, it's forgot or if not forgot, at least not thought about. Thank the Lord*!

Matt swung the cotton sack on his shoulder, and still talking, they walked toward the front gate, Luke leading his horse.

And he's just a boy. Not full-grown. Don't think about it. Nobody knows it, anyhow. Not Matt. Nobody.

They stopped at the front gate.

"I'll fetch this cotton to the barn directly," Matt said and lowered the sack to the ground. He leaned with one hand atop a fence post, the other fisted on his hip. Luke looked up at her and lifted his hat.

"Howdy, Tillie," he said, and smiled.

"Howdy, Luke," she said, and her throat tightened. "Y'all c'mon in, Matt, and I'll heat up the coffee."

"You've got time for coffee, ain't you Luke?" Matt said.

"I'm obliged, but I need to head on back home. Looks like it's gonna make up and rain anytime now."

"I was hoping it'd hold off a day or two," Matt said. "I got my corn pulled and in the crib but I still got cotton left to pick." He nodded at his field across the lane.

"I was hoping so, too, Matt," Luke said and turned to Button. "We got our corn in, but we got better'n five bales of cotton in a second picking, yet." He stepped into the stirrup iron, and gripping the pommel, he swung into the saddle. "We appreciate y'all's help, Matt." And pinching the brim of his hat at Tillie, he chucked up Button into a fast trot.

Matt watched a moment then walked through the gate and onto the porch. He draped his arm across her shoulders. She slipped her arm around his waist, and they watched Luke ride out the lane.

"What's the matter, sweetheart?" she said. "Luke looked serious."

"Retty's took a turn for the worst, and Luke fetched Doc Foley and is letting the folks know."

"Oh, my goodness. Poor Retty with them little young'uns, too. I hope she's not bad sick."

"I'm afraid she might be. I'll ride over there at first light," Matt said. "And Luke asked if some of 'em maybe could spend a night or two with us if it comes to that."

"Of course, they can," she said and pressed her swollen belly against his hip. "We've got plenny room, yet."

*

Retty's breath came fast and shallow. Thurston wiped her face with a cool, damp cloth. On the opposite side of the bed, Maud waved a palmetto fan back and forth, stirring the listless air. Morgan stood at one side of the cold fireplace with his hands clasped behind his back, his head bowed. Working a needle and thread, Amanda slowly rocked in the shaft of light that fell through the front window and sewed a button onto one of William's shirts. Martha came into the room ahead of Seth who carried the baby.

"Howdy, Uncle Morgan, Aunt Amanda." Seth said.

Amanda laid her sewing aside, and rocking to her feet, she went to them.

"Fine, Seth," Morgan said. "How's the weather looking?"

"Lemme have Nathan," Amanda said.

"Looks like clouds gathering to the southwest," Seth said as Amanda took the baby from his arms. "I figure we're gonna get a toad-strangler before the night's out."

"Look at this would you Morgan?" Amanda said. "If this baby ain't the spitting image of Seth Knox, I ain't ever seen it."

Thurston slowly rose from his chair.

"How's she doing, Pa Knox?" Martha whispered. She pulled the slipknot on her sunbonnet and took it off.

"Not good," Thurston said in a lowered voice. "Not good a-tall."

"What did Doc Foley say?" Seth asked.

"He said the blood poisoning was still spreading, but she has a chance if she can get some rest," Thurston said. "He left some medicine to help her rest, but she won't take it until she's seen Nathan and talked to you and Luke and the girls."

"Don't fret, Thurston," Retty said. Her voice trembled. "'All things work to the good of them...'"

"I know, Retty," Thurston said and patted her hand. "Seth and Martha are here. They've brought Nathan to see you."

"Bring him to me," Retty said and looked up at Amanda.

"Here's your grandma, Nathan," Amanda said and eased onto Thurston's bedside chair.

Retty reached up her hand, and the baby grasped her thumb.

"Stout as his pa, already," Retty said and closed her eyes.

"Are you hurting, Ma?" Maud said.

"Kiss Nathan on the lips for me."

"I'm gonna fix your medicine now, Ma," Maud said.

"Is Luke back yet?" Retty opened her eyes and looked about the bed.

"He'll be here directly, Ma," Seth said.

"Y'all oughta fix supper, ain't you Maud?" Retty said. "I wanna talk to Seth for a spell."

"Alright," Maud said and stood. "But I'm gonna mix your medicine while y'all visit."

"Milking time, ain't it, Thurston?" Retty said.

"I guess so," he said and started for the door.

"Me and Luke will milk and feed as soon as he gets here, Pa," Seth said.

"I'm obliged, son," Thurston said. "I'll go get the rinse water and milking pail ready for y'all."

"I'm gonna hitch up," Morgan said. "Me and Amanda are gonna stay the night at Pa's place, and William and Asa's already gone home with them."

"Yeah, Grandma and Grandpa and the boys was unloaded when we came by their place." Seth said. "And Doc Foley was giving Grandpa a hand unhitching his team."

Amanda bent over and kissed Retty's forehead.

"You rest easy, honey," she said, and carrying Nathan in her arms, Amanda followed Thurston and Morgan and Martha from the room. Seth sat in the bedside chair.

"Is there anything I can get for you, Ma?"

"No. But I wanna tell you, Seth, you're gonna have to help your pa look out for the young'uns, you and Luke and Maud and Sarah."

"You don't fret about the young'uns, Ma..."

The doorknob rattled and clicked, and the door opened. Luke balked on the threshold for a moment and wiped his feet, holding his hat in his hand. Reluctantly, as though forcing himself to move, he stepped into the room and shut the door.

"Here's Luke now," Seth said.

"Luke?" Retty said. She raised her hand, and Luke strode to the bed and took it in both of his.

"Ma, I'm sorry," Luke said. "I know I done wrong and caused you a worry."

"Luke, 'All have sinned and come short of the glory of God,' and Christ took the sins of all. All's forgot and forgave," Retty said. "You and Seth and Maud and Sarah are gonna have to help your pa look after Callie and Asa, now."

"Don't you worry 'bout that, Ma," Luke said. "You just worry 'bout getting better."

"Afraid I can't do that, son," Retty said, closing her eyes.

Luke looked at Seth and blinked his eyes. Maud came into the room carrying a drinking glass half-filled with a brownish colored liquid.

"Luke," she said. "Did you let Matt and Tillie know."

"Yeah, Matt said he'd be here at first light tomorrow and that they got plenny room for anybody to stay up there, if there's a need."

"Did you go by the Burgesses?"

“Uncle Richard said he’d get word to the Burgesses and Elder Purdy and the Odoms.”

“Y’all go on out to the kitchen and eat your supper,” Maud said. “Martha and Sarah are setting the table now.”

Seth and Luke shuffled toward the door as Thurston came in.

“The milking pails are by the back kitchen door for you and Luke, Seth,” he said.

“You don’t fret about none of the chores, Pa,” Seth said. “Me and Luke will do what needs to be done.”

“Is that your Ma’s potion, Maud?” Thurston said.

“Yes sir, I was about to give it to her.”

“You go on out to the kitchen and eat your supper, and I’ll give it to her.”

Maud handed him the glass of medicine, and he sat on the chair next to the bed. He leaned, slipped his arm under Retty’s shoulders, and raised her from the pillow. She opened her eyes and the corners of her mouth twitched attempting a smile. Thurston held the glass to her lips, and she drank. He lowered the glass.

“Bitter,” she said and nodded. He lowered the glass twice more to let her breathe before she emptied it then eased her back onto the pillow and wiped her mouth with a damp cloth.

“Now, you rest, honey,” he whispered. “I’m gonna be right here with you.” He kissed her lips and sat, his hand lightly resting on hers.

She lay in bed, her back straight and her chin up. “Like a lady,” her ma had said. Just like the night of the play-party, and she knew that she had loved him if not from the moment she first saw him leaning against the doorframe then at least from the first time he kissed her. A kiss he stole during the hog-hunter game.

*

She had been surprised and hesitant when her pa called Thurston's name as her hog-hunter partner, and Lum sat beside Mavis and didn't seem to notice.

Thurston bowed and held out his hand. She placed her hand in his, the first time their flesh touched, and she rose. Mavis sat in the chair to become the next "daughter" and held her fan over her mouth, but Retty saw the mischief playing in her eyes. The music began, and Retty took Thurston's arm, and he led her through the circle of hog-hunters and young women to an open window. A new couple sang and promenaded around her pa and Mavis.

"I'm Thurston Knox," he said.

"If you ain't, you're cheating," she said. She smiled at him and held his arm. "I'm Retty Tarroll."

"I done found out that your name's Retty Tarroll," he said. "I asked Horace Odom, and I'm mighty proud you picked me."

"I didn't pick you," she said. She waved her fan under her face, pleased he'd asked someone her name. "Pa did."

"Who'd you tell him to pick?"

"Nobody. He just usually always picks Lum."

"Lum?" he said. "You mean Lum Kendall?"

"He's the only Lum I'm acquainted with here," she said. "Besides, Lum happens to be a mighty nice feller."

"A nice feller?" He leaned until his forehead almost touched hers, the fan but a leaf between them. Softly he said, "A mighty nice feller, but is he your feller?"

She felt a flush spread over her throat and breast and looked up into his dark eyes. She swallowed, and Mavis and Lee Eustis joined them at the open window. Lee's lantern jaw gave him a horse-faced appearance. He was fun loving and about the best dancer around, and Mavis and Retty thought he was mighty nice, too.

"Howdy, Thurston," Lee said. "Ain't seen you in a coon's age." They shook hands, and Retty nodded to Mavis, who raised her fan to cover her smile.

"I ain't had no call to come over this way in a spell till Horace Odom come by the place this morning," Thurston said. "He said Mr. Rufe was throwing a big shindig over here tonight and the purtiest girls from Clemson to Salem was gonna be here."

"We're proud you came, Thurston," Mavis said. "I hope Horace didn't raise your expectation too high".

"Not a-tall," he said. "This is about the biggest fuss I was ever at."

Mavis smiled at Retty and lifted her eyebrows in a shrug.

"Let's sing," Retty said. Tugging Thurston's arm, she led him and Mavis and Lee to the rear of the circle of players waiting their turn to be paired. Laughter and clapping of hands followed Mr. Rufe's choice of hog-hunter for each of his "daughters."

Thurston whispered in Retty's ear, "I don't smoke nor chew and seldom drank liquor."

She lowered her head and smiled and squeezed his arm.

After all the players were paired, Hannah, who was fourteen, had joined the game, flushed and smiling and primping shyly. She faced her pa and laced fingers with him, and raising their joined hands, they made an arch of their arms. Retty remembered her excitement when at Hannah's age her pa first called her out among the older folks to help him make the bridge.

They all sang,

"Come under, come under,

"My honey, my love, my hearts above.

"Come under, come under,

"Below Galilee."

And Retty and Thurston led the other couples, bending and crouching, under the bridge.

After all had made the first passage, they were called through again by a second verse,

"We've caught you as a prisoner,

"My honey, my love, my heart's above.

"We've caught you as a prisoner,

"Below Galilee."

And her pa and Hannah momentarily captured her and Thurston in their arms, released them, then caught Mavis and Lee. The room filled with laughter and chatter and on their third passage, her pa and Hannah captured them in their arms, and everyone sang the last verse,

"Then hug 'er neat, and kiss 'er sweet,

"My honey, my love, my heart's above,

"Then hug 'er nice, and kiss 'er twice,

"Below Galilee."

She offered her cheek for the first kiss, but as she turned her head to offer the other cheek for the second kiss, he kissed her mouth. Their lips lingered, and her heart pounded.

"Whoa, son," her pa said and looked round at the laughing faces, his blue eyes full of fun. "We got us one of them there Hennessey Creek bobcats here tonight, folks!" He winked at Mavis. "What did you get my daughter paired up with, Mavis?" Then as Thurston sashayed with her away from the bridge amid the laughter, her pa said, "It's just a play-game, son!"

"Yes sir," Thurston said over his shoulder. "But I play for keeps, Mr. Rufe."

Arm in arm, they waited at the open window as Mavis and Lee Eustis made their final passage under the bridge amid hoots and guffaws. Her face and throat flushed in the warmth of the room and the nearness of Thurston Knox.

"I think Pa kinda favors you," she said.

"I'm mighty proud of that, but what I wanna know is, do you favor me?"

"I suppose I do."

"In that case, I'll be riding over this way next Saturday evening," he said.

"That'd be fine," she said. "Sometimes Lum comes by of a Saturday evening, too."

"Sometimes?"

"Yeah. Sometimes."

"I figure Lum'll have other things on his mind by then."

And Thurston was right. Lum was always a family friend and still worked for her pa parttime, but after, he never came to sit in the parlor and talk to her about buying the adjoining forty acres again.

*

And her ma and pa sat in the parlor on the other side of the wide hall, and she and Hannah swept the bedrooms. The doors were open for the spring breeze to freshen the house. Their voices weren't loud.

"I hoped for better for my girls, Rufe," her ma said. "I just can't help it. He's nothing."

"Rachel, I don't wanna hear any more of that kinda talk," her pa said. "I overheard what you said to Ludie Kendall after church last Sunday."

"I meant for you to hear it."

"Well, I won't have you saying such."

"I just want better for my girls, Rufe."

"Thurston Knox is a decent young feller, and his folks is honest and hardworking. Now, we're in business out here and if it gets around you're too proud for the Knoxs, other folks is gonna get to wondering if maybe you ain't too good for them too. That cotton gin and grist mill out there ain't the onliest ones in this part of the country."

"I just can't do it, Rufe. I can't go to Clemson and sign no paper for her to marry him."

"You don't have to," he said. "I'm her pa, and I'll do it, and you hold your peace, in this house and out."

And she held her peace, but she never really smiled at Retty again, not with the warm, embracing smile of the ma she remembered, and when she died, Retty wept for the ma she gave up when she married Thurston and for the shame and guilt that she felt because of her sometimes fleeting regrets for marrying him.

*

"Pa, go eat your supper," Sarah said. "I'll sit with Ma for a spell."

"Have Morgan and Amanda left yet?" he said. Stiffly, he came to his feet and rubbed his hips.

"Yes sir," she said. "They've been gone an hour or better, trying to beat the rain."

"I really ain't hungry, Sarah. I ate some cornbread and drunk a cup of pot liquor off the turnip greens after I fixed the milking pails for the boys."

"That ain't enough. You eat something, Pa."

"I won't be long," he said.

Chapter Twenty-two

In the kitchen-house, Onie washed the supper dishes, and Amanda dried and stacked them away in the china safe. Through the small back window, Amanda watched Morgan follow his pa to the barn to help him feed and milk. She slid the last plate into the safe and closed the door. Pensive, she turned to Onie.

"Ma, I'm terribly worried about Retty, and I'm afraid Thurston couldn't bear it if…"

Onie nodded her head, her brown eyes moist and shining.

"Thurston can bear whatever the Lord wills," she said. "It's all in His hands now, Amanda. Always has been. We've done all we can humanly do, and I've done my praying. I'm at peace. His will be done."

"I wish I had your faith, Ma."

"When you get to be my age, sugar, you're gonna unnerstand faith and love is about all that's left and might very well be all we ever had in the first place."

"Pray for me too, Ma."

"I always do, Amanda," Onie said and patted her arm. "Now, let's get outta this hot kitchen-house and go sit on the front porch where it's cooler and let the Lord take care of tomorrow, if it comes."

In the lane beyond the picket fence, William and Asa worked on their blowgun. Asa braced one end of the blowgun against the trunk of a red oak while William slid the grater-tipped hickory rod back and forth inside the cane, smoothing the bore.

"Do you think them boys is ever gonna finish that blowgun?" Amanda said.

"If they don't finish it soon, there ain't gonna be enough cane left to blow arrows through," Onie said and settled into her rocking chair near the end of the porch. She pulled her handkerchief and tin of snuff from her apron pocket and spread the handkerchief over her lap. Slowly, she twisted the lid from the snuff tin.

Jesus Christ, son of God, have mercy on a sinner like me.

Amanda sat in the rocking chair next to Onie and rested her head on the chair back.

Gathering thunderheads towered in the southwest and slowly blotted out the pitiless sun. Rain frogs chirped their frantic yearning as the evening woods cooled. An owl floated out of the darkening trees and landed in the far end of the lane beyond where the boys worked and ruffled its feathers and scratched and flapped its wings like a chicken until dust rose in a whirlwind. Onie eyed the owl, suspicious of the bird's intention toward her chickenyard as her tongue worked the snuff until it lay easy against her gums and cheek.

"Look out, Mr. Owl," she said. "You gittin' mighty close to the chickenyard. Pa'll bust your tail feathers."

"I've heard tell that if you see an owl dust hisself it brings bad luck," Amanda said.

"Why, Amanda. You're a Christian woman and your husband's a min'ster of the Gospel. Don't tell me you put any stock in such heathen idees as that?"

"No, ma'am, I don't. I'm just saying I've heard tell some folks believe that it's bad luck."

"Well, I never believed any dumb creature had anything to say about what's gonna happen or what's not gonna happen. The Scriptures say time and chance snares all of us, but if that mister flops around in that dust out there too long and Pa gets his shotgun, it's gonna appear like dusting hisself is bad luck for that owl."

Thunder growled within the gathering clouds.

"Sounds like it's gonna make up and rain sure," Onie said.

"Yes, ma'am, it does," Amanda said. Then raising her voice, she said, "William, you boys c'mon up here on the porch!"

"Ah, Ma."

"Mind what I say, now. There's apt to be lightening in them thunderheads, and it's about to set in to raining."

"But I'll allow, many strange things happen in this life, sugar," Onie said. "Plenny that a body can't rightly see, or hear, for that matter, and if you do see or hear them, you don't always unnerstand what it is. But I'm speaking of things that ain't got nothing to do with some dumb creature like an owl."

"William, y'all c'mon up here," Amanda said as the boys dawdled near the gate. "Don't make me call y'all again."

The hinges squeaked as the gate swung open and shut. William hooked the latch chain, and suddenly, the boys broke and raced up the steps, scrambled across the porch, and dropped to the floor, their backs against the wall of the house.

"You boys settle down!" Amanda said.

Onie leaned across the arm of her chair toward the end of the porch, braced her lips with forked fingers, and spat into the yard. Deliberately, she picked up her handkerchief, wiped her mouth, and again, she spread it over her lap. She raised her hand to her bosom, and her fingertips read her neck-beads.

"Many strange and contrary things happen in this life," she said, staring down the lane into her memory past where the owl had dusted itself.

*

George and his older brother, Dave, had tied up in fisticuffs down on the bank of the Hennessey Creek late one January morning a few months before Dave moved his family down on the Red River. They were killing hogs and came upon a disagreement over something. Sometimes when she went over it in her head about all that had happened, maybe late at night waiting for sleep or in the sunshine picking beans in her garden, she had vague glimpses and inklings of things that never quite came into full view. She never rightly understood what their row was all about.

They were brothers and loved like brothers, but their temperaments were too similar and maybe too dissimilar, too. Dave was quiet and slight of build but taller than George, George being thicker and heavier by then, and more outspoken. A body always knew when George Knox was afoot, but nobody was ever sure about Dave until they looked around and sort of fell into his washed colored eyes. Pale blue but a color hard to describe. Not keen and clear like George's and Jim's. Some folks say his eyes were gray, but they looked blue to her, pale blue, like old blue patterned china after the blue has been scoured and soaped and almost washed out, like a hazy sky.

Dave Knox was the only human being she was ever afraid of after she grew up. She had sense enough to get out of George's way whenever he threw one of his mean fits, but that was prudence, smart afraid. His fits passed sooner or later, and everything was alright. But with Dave Knox it was like being afraid of a rattlesnake. A particular look or smile crossing Dave's face chilled the bones just like the sound of a startled insect's wings buzzing in dry leaves did. Blinding fear, bone deep, rattlesnake afraid. Fear that augers in the bones. Fear that can't be looked at nor looked away from. Fear that dries the marrow.

She was around Dave Knox and often for a certainty, he being George's brother and Betsy, his wife, being sweet and gentle. She hadn't felt fear like that again since the letter came saying Dave was dead, shot from his horse and killed in a row over a hog dog and Betsy left with seven young'uns. Four of the young'uns were nearly grown by then, but life is hard on a young widow or an old widow for that matter. Sometimes she thought that either must be nigh as hard as being a wife.

She heard them down at the hog pen, loud and cussing. It wasn't a half of a quarter-mile from the kitchen steps to the hog pen on the high bank of Hennessey Creek. Henry Jurgens and Hugh Odom had ridden in with Dave at first light to help George with killing hogs, but Jim had tarried.

"By golly, gall dang you, Dave!" George said, and she knew that Jim wasn't there, yet. He being the oldest, the most sensible of the three, usually held George from fighting, unless Jim had had a drink of liquor.

"I didn't know it was you, George," Dave said. "But if it was you, you dawdled, durn your hide!"

"Gall dang you, Dave," George said. "Jim's commander. You ain't!" And she knew they were going fisticuffs, and that Jim wasn't there and that he had never been commander of anything that she ever knew, and she was scared.

Erin was just a baby, then, and Thurston, not yet two, and George Knox down on the high bank fighting Dave Knox, and Jim wasn't there yet. And she knew Dave in a way that Betsy didn't know him. Maybe even like George and Jim didn't know him, and them going to lodge meetings at least once a month and sometimes every other week or going foxhunting. Before the War, George didn't give a whit for such things as lodges and foxhunts.

"A feller can't eat no dang fox," he would say to Jim, but after the War, lots of things changed, but still, she thought she knew Dave better than any of them. That's what she thought then, being afraid. But she knew better, later. There was still plenty she didn't know. Many strange things happened in life that a body couldn't rightly put a handle on, but she knew now that they knew him, and he knew them, and they knew each other, being brothers, all the same blood, and her just a sister-in-law, a wife, and they were men and had all been soldiers together fighting the Yankee like he was a wildcat in the cow lot, shedding his blood, and him theirs, sleeping on the ground, sharing grub, coffee, fire and blanket and fear and madness. Fighting the wildcat until the last calf was dead and winter coming on and no meat nor shoes for the young'uns. There was a bond forged there that was different from the bond any preacher or justice of the peace could hammer, a different kind of bond but maybe as strong.

But she was afraid then. George and Dave down there going fisticuffs, and Jim had tarried. Two weeks earlier, she had seen Dave Knox murder a man, and more.

*

"I'm gonna take the boys in, now, Ma," Amanda said. "It's time I got 'em washed up and in bed."

"Y'all go ahead, sugar," she said. "I'm gonna sit here and enjoy the evening cool a little longer." She rested her head on the back of the rocking chair and watched as the clouds grew darker over the treetops.

Chapter Twenty-three

Back then, Shady Grove Church met once a month on second Sundays because Brother Cicero Inglish was one of only three Methodist ministers riding circuit in Okaloosa Parish west of Clemson, and he served four churches. During the afternoon singing, Erin, who was still nursing, began to fret, so she left Thurston with George and eased outside to quiet her. Horses, mules and oxen and wagons and carts crowded the wide lane in front of the church house. The day was clear and blue with a dishrag of a cloud here and there, and the sun shone mellow in the winter chill.

She stepped out into the yard and walked to the side of the church house humming and rocking Erin in her arms. A picket fence around the church house kept woods stock out of the yard, and Sister Inglish worked hard to keep it pretty. Cape jasmines and roses flowered in the spring and summer and camellias in the winter, which kept their green foliage even after they dropped their blooms. The Inglishs had brought the camellias from Washington Parish, where Brother Inglish had ridden circuit until he was appointed to the Okaloosa Parish circuit, and she stood among those camellias, more or less out of sight. Naturally, she glanced about to see that she was alone before she began to unbutton her bodice to nurse Erin and saw two men beyond the lane in the edge of the woods. It wasn't unusual for folks to be outside of the church house during the singing service, or during the preaching for that matter, but she looked closer out of curiosity, just to mark who they were.

She recognized Dave Knox and Tom Jenkins. Dave had an arm around Tom's shoulders, their heads almost touching, and talking friendly like it appeared to her. Tom looked up and saw her and kind of nodded, still listening to Dave. Dave glanced up, too, but he looked toward the front of the church house and didn't see her. She stood and watched not really knowing why other than Erin had quit fretting by then. She didn't hear their words above the singing coming from the congregation, but she couldn't turn away, and she never understood why she couldn't. Suddenly, quicker than a thought, Dave pulled a knife from under his coat and stabbed Tom under the brisket.

She stood breathless, unable to move, trying to fix in her mind what she was seeing.

Dave held Tom's coat lapel and lifted him off the ground on his knife blade three times. When he stabbed Tom, Dave turned his back to the church house, so she didn't see his face, but Tom faced her, looking over Dave's shoulder. His mouth gaped and rounded like he was howling, but he didn't make a sound that she could hear, and it seemed he looked her directly in the eye while Dave gripped his coat and bounced him on the blade of his knife. Tom looked at her all the while, kind of stiff and jerking both at the same time. Directly, Tom sagged, and Dave eased him to the ground, like he was helping an old man to sit down then stretched him out gentle like, and she couldn't see Tom's face anymore.

Later, she thought that might not have been how it was, Tom looking her in the eye. That may have come from dreams she had afterward, peculiar dreams, because in the moment of his dying, it seemed to her that Tom Jenkins looked at her and loved her and loved Dave, and she loved Tom and Dave, but Dave Knox didn't love either one of them.

Whether in a dream or not, she felt she had witnessed grace in the horror of it and would never forget it. It was pure grace that a fellow could love the man who murdered him. A mystery, a foreshadowing or maybe even a retelling, and she shuddered to remember how Dave had stood outside that grace and prayed that he went down on his knees before his Lord and Savior before he died, before that fellow killed him in the row over that hog dog. But she knew for a certainty if that fellow hadn't killed Dave, Dave Knox would've killed him, sure.

Dave stood over Tom for what seemed like a long while, the bloody knife in his hand. Then with a quick glance over his shoulder, he saw her standing among the camellias. He nodded politely and leaned and wiped his knife blade on Tom's lapel and slipped it back under his coat. Bending over, he took a hold on the back of Tom's collar and dragged his body from the edge of the lane into the woods and stretched him under a hawthorn bush. In the casual way he did it, it seemed to her like he dragged him into the woods, not so much to conceal murder or hide the body, as to get him from underfoot.

She felt a weakness in her bladder as Dave, with steady, long strides came across the lane toward her. He pulled his handkerchief from his coat pocket and wiped his hands as he walked. She wanted to run into the church house, but it seemed to her as though her strength had drained from her legs through her feet into the ground. She hummed the hymn that welled from the church house and trembled, swaying Erin in her arms. Dave stopped at the picket fence less than five paces from where she stood and looked at her over the camellia bushes and doffed his hat. His right coat sleeve was sopping wet almost to the elbow with Tom's blood.

"Onie, tell Betsy I heard my brindle cur bayed on a hog down in the Hennessey swamp and that I went to call him off before he got hog cut," he said. "Tell her that I'll walk home through the woods, so she'll have to bring the wagon." He looked her dead in the eye. "And if what you seen here today ever passes your lips, I'll give you the same dose as I gave him."

Dave's blue-white eyes waited until she nodded then he turned and walked into the woods past the hawthorn bush where Tom Jenkins's body lay on God's own cooling board. Sniffling, she hugged Erin to her bosom and paced around the church house half a dozen times. When the pounding of her heart had slowed and she had calmed enough, she went back inside the church house and sat down on the pew behind Betsy. With her eyes closed, she prayed and prayed harder. Finally, she leaned forward and whispered into Betsy's ear. In a calm and natural whisper, she said what Dave had told her to say. After services, Sam Foley found poor Tom Jenkins's body.

Oh, the keening! Almost forty years on and in the quiet of night, she sometimes heard Ada Jenkins keening over her husband's dead body and the young'uns squalling. It still tore her heart. Why would Dave want to kill Tom Jenkins? It was a mystery to her. Unless maybe it was because Dave Knox was the meanest man that ever drew the breath of life.

On Tuesday afternoon, they buried Tom at Shady Grove Cemetery not more than a hundred steps from where Dave killed him. Henry Jurgens and Hugh Odom and Sam Foley stood with George, Jim, and Dave Knox as pallbearers. They all had gone off and fought together in the War, and Dave had killed him, but no one knew that but her and Dave, and as long as Dave Knox was alive, the truth of it never passed her lips.

Brother Inglish delivered a fine graveside sermon. She didn't remember all he said, but in his closing prayer, he prayed for the soul of Judas. She had never heard anybody make that prayer before, but since, whenever she prayed, she tried to remember to pray for the soul of Judas Iscariot. By the time Brother Inglish said Amen, there wasn't a dry eye in the cemetery. She saw Dave Knox pull out his handkerchief, and she knew that even though he was a murderer, he wasn't a man to lie or put on a false face. He murdered a man, who was his friend for God only knows what reason, but there was no doubt in her mind that he wiped honest tears from his eyes. Those were strange, contrary times.

Even the sheriff, Caleb Wicker, drove out in his buggy just for Tom's funeral. Folks say he was pocket-change for the Jayhawkers that ran roughshod over Okaloosa Parish from the end of the War until 'sixty-nine. As a rule, Sheriff Wicker wasn't concerned about thieving and murder and such, but he seemed to take a particular interest in poor Tom and his murder. He mingled with the folks and asked plenty of questions about who had seen Tom and who had talked to him that day and something about beans. Had he planted beans? Or was he going to plant beans? Or some such nonsense. She later asked George what that was all about, and he said Wicker had to ask something, being the sheriff. But she thanked the Lord, the sheriff didn't say a word to her, so she didn't have to tell a lie. That spring, about the middle of May, Caleb Wicker was found slumped in his buggy at the fork of the Buskin and Salem Roads with a pistol ball in his brain.

Several evenings later, Sam Foley rode up while she was in the kitchen-house fixing supper. He and George sat on the front porch, and they talked in hushed voices. She eased down the dogtrot hall to the front door just to make sure nothing serious was wrong. She was really quiet because she didn't want to disturb them, and she overheard some of their words.

"Well, George, they found Sheriff Wicker shot dead down at the forks. It looks to me like he found that white bean he was looking for," Sam remarked. It sounded downright cold-blooded to her, seeing how folks kept turning up dead just a couple of miles from their front gate, first Tom Jenkins and now Sheriff Wicker.

"It appears he did, Sam," George said, and Sam chuckled. He was a doctor, and she allowed that he was a fine doctor, but Sam Foley had a heart like a peach stone, hard, wrinkled and sharp as a needle.

*

No one ever knew for a certainty who murdered Caleb Wicker. Some folks pointed the finger at George Knox, but Onie had her own suspicions, which she figured were just as well left unsaid, but she knew for a certainty, by the witness of her own eyes, who killed Tom Jenkins.

And George fought with him behind their house on the high bank of Hennessey Creek. She knew they were brothers, but so were Cain and Abel. Being afraid to wait any longer for Jim, she took Erin in her arms and Thurston by the hand and walked and ran to the hog pen. George and Dave had their coats off and their shirtsleeves rolled above their elbows. In her first glance, she looked to see if Dave had his knife. He didn't. Their guns and knives and coats lay in a pile on the ground next to the hog pen. Two black sows and three spotted barrows ran round inside the pen grunting and squealing every time Dave or George lunged at the other. Blood was smeared under George's nose, and a knot swelled on Dave's cheek. Henry Jurgens and Hugh Odom stood to one side watching.

"Stop 'em, Henry!" she said.

"No ma'am. This is between them, Onie. I got no stake in it." She looked at Hugh.

He shook his head and said, "No, ma'am. I come to a hog killing not to fisticuffs, unless one of 'em was to jump on me."

"George!" Jim said. She hadn't noticed Jim ride up. "George! Dave!" Jim swung from his saddle and stepped between them standing face to face with George.

"Dave, go home," Jim said over his shoulder. "Get your coat and pistol and go home."

"You get, Dave!" George said through gritted teeth. "Dang you! I've always pulled my own wagon. I never needed your durn hand!"

"He was way passed his time and dangerous!" Dave said. "You're my brother, George, and I'll grant you've got spunk, but you ain't seen the elephant yet." He put on his hat and pulled on his coat and slipped his knife and pistol under his belt.

"Y'all hush, now," Jim said. He nodded toward Onie, and she nodded back.

"If I ever see you again, Dave Knox, I'll kill you as soon as I would a dang Jayhawker!"

"I figure that'll give me several years," Dave said and gave a snort.

"Gall dang you, Dave!" George lunged, but Jim caught him pinning his arms to his sides.

"Go home, Dave!" Jim said. "Now!"

Dave mounted his horse and looked at her.

"Morning, Onie," he said, and pinching the crown of his hat, he lifted it clear of his head. A smile touched his lips, and his blue-white eyes held her. He waited until she nodded her head, and still holding his hat lifted in his right hand, Dave wheeled his horse and kicked him into a gallop up Hennessey Creek, through the tall cypress trees toward his place two miles distance.

"I hope I never lay eyes on your face again, Dave Knox! If I do, God as my witness, I'll kill you!"

But they saw each other one last time.

One evening that June after she had cleared the supper table and put Thurston and Erin to bed, she and George sat on the porch trying to catch a dying breeze. A twig of a moon hung in the southwest, shining through the dark pine branches. At the far end of the lane, a whippoorwill whistled sharp as a distant star. Just under the dry chirr of seventeen year locusts, hoof-beats drummed in the dust of the road.

The horse stopped. Saddle leather squeaked like when a rider stands in the stirrups and turns to left or right. George leaned forward in his chair. She saw the horse and rider, dark as a shadow, and something pale, bigger than just a hand waved back and forth above the rider's head. He ventured up the lane. In those hard, strange days folks were ever watchful.

"Get me my shotgun, Onie. Now, Onie. Hurry!"

She scrambled into the darkened front room and fumbled for the gun that leaned in the corner next to the fireplace and shuffled back to the porch. George grabbed it. He hadn't taken his eyes off the rider.

"You stay indoors, Onie." George seldom used her given name after Thurston was born. He called her Ma unless it was in the way of a serious nature. She stepped back into the house, and George slipped out to the gate. The latch chain chinked, and the iron hinges squeaked, and he went outside the yard fence to wait.

The rider pulled up twenty paces or so beyond George, and she saw that he was waving a white handkerchief over his head. George nodded and motioned him in with the barrel of his gun. Dusk hung like a veil between the men and her, but she saw that the rider wore a duster and wide brim straw hat. They exchanged words, but she couldn't make out what was being said. George stepped back, and the rider swung down from the saddle. They clasped hands and hugged.

"Ma! It's Dave come home. Kill the fatted calf!"

She stepped through the door onto the porch.

"C'mon out to the kitchen, Dave, and I'll warm up supper for you and wake the young'uns," she said, and her heart pounded. "They'd wanna see you, too." She felt succored in her fear.

"No, no, Onie," he said. "Don't bother yourself with me. I have a ways to ride yet. Jim's expecting me to sleep over at his place tonight. I'll be headed back down to the Red River in the morning, and I just figured to say hello to y'all before I left. Give Thurston and Erin a kiss for me when they wake in the morning."

From the dark beyond the gate, their voices murmured across the yard to the porch, but she couldn't make out the words they said, but she knew they had settled their difference. She felt good about Dave then, about him stopping off and patching things up with George because she knew George, being the younger, wouldn't have, couldn't have gone to Dave and him feeling Dave had slighted him or belittled him about whatever misunderstanding they had. She had to allow that in spite of his meanness, Dave Knox was a good brother.

Directly, he climbed on his horse and turned out the lane, and she watched and listened until the horse and rider, and the soft plopping of hooves in the summer dust were soaked up by the maddening chirr of the locusts. The iron hinges squeaked as George came back into the yard and closed the gate, and up the Hennessey, from near Dave's old place, a screech owl's scream cut the night. The hair stood on the nape of her neck, and for a moment, silence fixed the darkness like it must in the coffin after friends and family have gone home.

*

In early fall he rode up the lane for the first time. She had put Thurston and Erin to bed and sat alone on the porch in the dying light waiting for George to come home from one of his lodge meetings. At first, she thought the rider was George and began to rise from her chair, but something about him, maybe the way he slouched in the saddle, made her to understand it wasn't George. She eased back into her seat, and he stopped his horse about twenty paces outside the front gate and sat without moving, without sound. She sat very still thinking maybe he hadn't seen her and squinted, trying to make out his shadowy figure. About the time she decided to run into the house and bolt the doors, the rider and horse faded into the distant line of trees and was gone. But it wasn't his last visit. Sometimes he rode up, climbed from the saddle, and walked through the front gate, and the latch chain chinked, and the iron hinges squeaked, but no one was ever there as far as a body could see. Once she went so far as to dab the hinges with hog lard and swing the gate back and forth until it swung as quietly as a baby's sigh, and that very evening he rode up, climbed from his horse and the latch chain chinked, and the hinges squalled. He always came on a clear night with just a twig of a moon curled in a sky full of stars, but never on as much as a quarter, whether on the wax or on the wane and always on a night when George was away at a lodge meeting or on a fox or coon hunt.

He wasn't just any spirit either. She believed it was Caleb Wicker. Some folks said George Knox killed him on the dark of a new moon at the fork of the Buskin and Salem Roads. She knew in her heart that George didn't kill Caleb Wicker and had her own ideas about who did.

But George Knox never paid much mind to things like a horse and rider that wasn't there, riding up the lane at dusk dark or just after dark, and the sound of the gate opening and closing but no one ever walking up onto the porch, like they were holding back, like maybe they were afraid to approach the honest light of a Christian home. George didn't believe in ghosts and such.

"But what is a ghost, Pa," she said, "if it ain't the shades and shadows buried in a body's heart?"

"Shah!" he said. "Your heart's a living, beating thing, Ma. It ain't no grave!" And she was satisfied that was the very thing he couldn't understand, didn't want to understand.

"That's just so, Pa," she said. "The heart ain't a grave, and it wa'n't intended to hold still-living yearnings and fears," thinking, *Oh, how we bury our quick-dead secrets, how we weep and cry over them and say our prayers over them and bid our final good-byes, but they never die. They suckle our heart's blood, and at odd moments, like when the fragrance of some flower almost forgot tweaks our nose or when a hazy sky takes on a peculiar pale blue tint, the heart gapes like an open grave and some quick-dead secret steps out plain as the ghost of old Samuel.*

"Shaw!" George said.

"Why, Pa," she said. "If we could see all that's buried in the human heart, it'd burn the very eyes from our skull."

"I'll pay notice if ever there's something there to prove the sounds are anything more than your own addled musings late of an evening," he said, "waiting for me to come home from hunting or running my traps, addled musing rolling like echoes up the Hennessey Creek, maybe even remembering the sound of Dave riding up the lane for the last time."

*

The chair rockers groaned over the worn porch planks. Onie packed her dip of snuff with the tip of her tongue and stared at the encroaching evening beyond the gate. Lightning bloomed and faded among the thunderheads, etching the dark pine tops in brief light.

"Many strange things happen in this life," she said, her soft voice emerging from the silence.

Fat raindrops burst on the board shingles, and thunder rumbled beyond the pines. The kitchen-house door opened and closed. Muffled voices talked in hushed tones.

Pa and Morgan bringing in the evening milk. She slowly leaned across the arm of her chair toward the end of the porch, and bracing her lips with forked fingers, she spat at the darkness.

PART IV

Chapter Twenty-four

October 4, 1906

"Steady, Nubbin," Matt said. He buttoned his slicker and turned the collar up to cover his neck and tugged down the brim of his hat. Taking the reins, he led the gelding from the barn into the gray October drizzle and through the lot gate into the lane.

The rain had come during the night, furious and bright. Thunder rolled from the south and west and crashed directly over the roof, it seemed, rattling windows and doors. The wind dashed rain against the roof and the walls of the house.

"Matt!" Tillie said and shook him awake. "It's coming a storm."

He jumped from bed, and fast stepping through the house, he checked the doors and windows to make sure they were firmly fastened against the weather. Back in their bedroom he looked out the window toward his cornfield. But even under the glow of the running lightning, he couldn't see the cornstalks through the slashing rain. Slipping back into bed, he silently prayed that the rain was a short thunderstorm and not an early onset of winter. Tillie clung to him pulling her warm, swollen body close.

"Don't plan on going over to Retty's in the morning if this weather don't break, sweetheart," she murmured.

"I've gotta go, Tillie," he said. "You know Retty's as much my ma as she is my sister, and I'm afraid she's in a bad way. Besides, I wanna make sure the folks all know they're welcome to stay over here."

"Be sure and tell Seth and Martha to come. I so wanna hold a baby. I can't hardly wait to hold ours. Can you, Matt? Can you hardly wait?"

He slipped his arm under her shoulders, and pulling her close, he laid his palm on her belly.

*

Riding out the lane toward the Buskin Road, he looked over his rain drenched cotton field. The sopping, mud-spattered cotton hung in strings from the open hulls. Hunching his shoulders under the heavy mist, he set his eyes on the lane ahead. Rivulets ran from the road into the ditch where Thurston had sat on his horse last March sowing doubts, talking down to him while he propped on the rail fence. If Thurston hadn't ridden over the morning after he ran Luke from his house and said what he said, he wouldn't have known what he knows he doesn't know and can never know, can never allow himself to know.

Thurston had no call putting in his spoke. He should've just stayed out of it. But he didn't, and Matt wondered what would've happened if he hadn't forgotten the ax that afternoon and ridden back to the house to get it. Just as he rode out of the woods, he saw Luke break and run toward the house. He thought Tillie must have called out, maybe hurt herself, and he'd kicked Nubbin into a gallop. He went through the back gate and heard Luke say, "My

God, Tillie, I'm burning!" And when he stepped into the doorway, he saw Tillie slap his hand,

and say, "Go draw the wash water." And he wondered what might have happened if he had been five minutes later coming back to fetch the ax, and if nothing more had happened between Tillie and Luke than what he saw in the kitchen, how come Thurston was so worried?

And not just worried but scared. Had Luke told more, and Thurston was afraid Tillie had told him more, too?

But Tillie threw the burnt pies out in the yard and came back to bed, soft and yielding, and after, he said, "I didn't hurt you did I, Tillie?"

"No, sweetheart." She stroked his cheek with her fingertips, her brown eyes shiny, and her hair smelling fresh-washed and smoky. "You felt nice. I think we made a baby."

"Can you tell such as that, right off?"

"A woman kinda knows, I think," she said. "The way it feels inside. Besides, if we didn't, we can try again tomorrow. We gotta have our babies don't we, Matt?" And she slipped her arm across his chest.

The next morning, he rowed up the cornfield, thinking about Tillie and about them making a baby in her stomach, her smooth, warm stomach. And how he hadn't hurt her but had pleased her and how her eyes shined as she sat beside him at breakfast, her hand touching his wrist, and talked and laughed. Then, Thurston rode up and unraveled the twine from his little bag of doubts the same as he would've opened a sack of flour.

Searching Thurston's eyes, he had gripped the top fence rail and felt his shoulders and legs wilt and vomit rise in his throat. And when Thurston pulled his horse around and cantered out the lane, he choked back an urge to run to the house, to ask Tillie, to look into her eyes and ask her straight out. He slowly walked to the plow, stumbled on a clod in the freshly plowed dirt, and with trembling hands, he unhitched the mule. He left the singletree swinging from the tongue of the plow stock and hung the trace rings on the hames, and grabbing a handful of mane, he swung himself astride the mule's back. He had to know. He had to look at her and know. And in his head, he asked the question and heard her answers over and over as he rode to the house.

On the one hand, she'd say, "Oh, Matt, I so hoped you'd never ask, that you'd never have to know." And she looked at him, tears in her eyes, and he didn't believe her. He knew the question had wounded her and her answer was meant to cut him, but he'd asked the question and couldn't take it back.

Then again, she'd say, "Oh, Matt. Don't you know you're the only man that's ever touched me like that! How could you think such a thing? Didn't I tell you yesterday that he'd never pulled anything like that before? That I would've told you if he had? How could you, Matt? How could you make a baby in me and then ask me if I'm an unfaithful wife? Will you ask me this every day for the rest of my life?" And there were no tears, only loss and sadness in her eyes, and she turned and went into their bedroom and quietly shut the door.

At the back gate, he slid off the mule and walked into the yard. He knew whatever answer she gave him was the only answer he'd ever have, and she'd given it yesterday: "Don't you know I would've told you if he had." As he mounted the steps and walked across the porch, he heard her humming. His heart leapt at the sound.

"You finished up in the cornfield, sweetheart?" she said. She smiled over her shoulder, her face flushed in the kitchen heat, and kept working a lump of dough on the floured table.

"Not yet," he said and walked to the table beside her. "Thurston just rode by to talk."

"About Luke?"

"He made his regrets about the way Luke acted, and I made mine about what I'd said to Luke."

"Well, it's best forgot," she said. He watched her as she rubbed flour over the rolling pin. "Luke's just a big old overgrown boy, and I'm sure he's ashamed of what he did. You want me to pour you some coffee?" She laid the rolling pin aside and turned to face him. Her soft, guileless eyes sought his, and suddenly, he felt ashamed of his thoughts.

"No, I don't want coffee." He smiled and settled his hands on her waist. "What're you making, darling?"

"Raisin pies," she said. Her warm voice touched his throat.

"Well, don't put 'em in the oven yet," he said, pulling her to him. She tiptoed, wrapped her arms around his neck, marking him with flour, and pressed her body to his.

"Oh, Matt!"

*

Despair weighed on his shoulders, a quiet, turning despair, ever turning in his head until an ingrained sadness lay softly at the corners of his mouth and eyes.

When I looked in the door and saw Luke touching her, her face looked pleased, like she enjoyed what he was doing. But she pushed him away and told him to quit and never saw me until I came through the door. But I saw her face and how pleased she looked. My fault! I should have tended to her more.

He peered up into the roiling, gray clouds and knew he'd never know. With his open palm, he wiped the rain from his face and bumped Nubbin with his heels.

*

Gray light pushed through the windowpanes. The mantel clock ticked, and rain dripped from the eaves. Muffled voices and morning sounds seeped through the thin walls. In the kitchen-house, the oven door clanked open and shut, and a chair bumped and scraped the floor in a back room. Each sound and voice was familiar to Retty. She caught stray words, fragments of kitchen talk, "skillet," "flour," and "coffee," and recognized the voices of Martha, Sarah, and Seth, but she couldn't make out a complete phrase or sentence. A fire snapped and hissed in the fireplace, and the dank, cool air smelled of woodsmoke and bacon. Surprised that she'd lived through another night, she opened her eyes and looked up at Maud.

"Are you awake, Ma?" Maud said. She stooped over her ma and lifted her head and propped her up with a pillow. "I want you to try and take some broth."

She picked up a bowl and stirred it with a spoon, and Retty weakly smiled and slowly opened her mouth.

*

"Luke, you better get the milking done, son," Thurston said and set the pails on the kitchen shelf.

"I'm ready, Pa," Luke said and drained his coffee cup.

"I'm gonna help you with the milking and feeding," Seth said. "Then I'll go home and do my own chores."

"I'll go help you, too," Luke said.

"No, you stay here, Luke. I'll ride Button, and it won't take me long."

As Luke and Seth rose from the table, Maud came into the kitchen carrying a bowl and spoon and an empty water glass.

"Did your ma eat anything?" Thurston said.

"Not much," Maud said. Her eyes were red-rimmed. "She took her medicine and a couple of spoons of broth. That's all."

"You go lie down for a spell, Maud," he said. "I'll sit with your ma, and Sarah and Martha can finish up in here. You look about tucker out."

"I guess I am," she said and set the bowl and glass by the dishpan.

"Pa, should I hitch up and drive over to Grandpa's and fetch Asa after we milk and feed?" Luke said. He took his hat from a nail near the back door and pushed it on his head.

"Let's wait awhile, Luke," he said. "I figure your Uncle Morgan'll be over here later, rain or shine, and he'll bring Asa. If he happens not to then you'll have to go."

"Don't bother about it, Luke," Seth said and put on his hat. "After I do my chores, I'll stop by Grandpa's an' get him if Uncle Morgan happens not to come."

"Well, either way, y'all clear outta the kitchen," Sarah said. "We ain't got room to turn around in here."

They went out the back door, their hats slanted to the light rain and long-stepped among the rain puddles to the barn.

"I'll milk, if you'll feed," Seth said.

"That suits me," Luke said and handed him the milking pails.

"Looks like somebody's coming down the Buskin Road," Seth said and nodded toward a horse and rider trudging through the misting rain. The rider had his head down and his hat pulled low over his face.

"Looks like Matt," Luke said. "Yeah, it is. I'll go open the lot gate for him if you'll open the barn door." And he splashed across the dung-muddy barn lot and swung open the gate.

"Over here, Matt!" he called and waved.

Raising his head, Matt bumped Nubbin's sides with his heels, and Nubbin cantered through the gate, his hooves spattering Luke with muddy dung. Luke swung the gate shut and latched it and followed Matt into the barn.

"Howdy, Matt," Seth said. Matt stepped from the stirrup, and they shook hands. "Looks like you was about to get wet."

"That's a fact," he said. He slapped his dripping hat against his leg.

"How's Tillie faring?" Seth asked. "Is she getting grumpy, yet?"

"No," Matt said. "Not a-tall."

Luke scrapped muddy spatter from his britches leg with a corncob and tossed it out the open door.

"Howdy, Matt."

"Luke," Matt said. He shook Luke's extended hand and turned to Seth. "How's Retty this morning, Seth?"

"It don't look good, Matt," Seth said. "She told me and Luke yesterday that she ain't gonna make it."

"I was a-hoping and praying she wouldn't be so bad," Matt said, and pressing his lips together, shook his head.

"You go on up to the house and see Ma, Matt," Luke said and laid his hand on Matt's saddle. "I'll take care of Nubbin for you."

"I'm obliged," Matt said.

"Will he take feed?" Luke said.

"You might give him a ear of corn against this chill," Matt said.

"You go on up to the house, Matt," Seth said. "Ma'll be anxious to see you."

*

"She's doing right well, Sarah," Matt said. He hung his slicker and hat at the backdoor, and water dripped to the floor and began to puddle, then drained out a crack between the floorboards. "I guess we're both gittin' fidgety and anxious."

"It ain't much longer, is it?" Martha said and hugged his neck.

"Sometimes before Christmas is what they tell me. How's this little feller doin'?" He leaned and kissed Nathan's forehead.

"Gitting bigger and heavier ever' day," Martha said.

"Can I get you some breakfast, Matt?" Sarah said. Drying her hands on her apron, she crossed the kitchen and kissed his cheek.

"No," he said. "I ate a bite before I left the house, but I figure I could tolerate a cup of coffee."

"Stand by the cookstove and dry yourself," Sarah said. "I'll pour your coffee."

"Seth said Retty's not doing well," he said. He stood to one side of the stove and held his hands over the heat, and rubbing them together, he watched Sarah pour his coffee. *She has Retty's blue eyes and auburn hair. Maud and Seth are brown-eyed, but Luke is blue-eyed like Sarah.*

"Maud sat with her last night and said she slept some better," Sarah said. "But she didn't eat much this morning."

Asa and Callie are brown-eyed.

"Here's your coffee," Sarah said.

"This'll warm me up," he said, and tentatively raised the steaming cup to his lips and sipped. "What did Doc Foley say?"

"He said the blood poisoning is spreading," Sarah said. "But said as strong as Ma is, she's got a chance."

"Is Thurston with her now?" he said and wondered what his and Tillie's young'uns will look like, who their child will favor.

"Yeah," Sarah said. "He just took Callie in to see her for a minute."

"I guess I better go in to see her," he said. *I'm as blue-eyed as Retty. Tillie's got brown eyes and hair. Not as dark as Thurston's.*

The door opened, and Thurston followed Callie into the kitchen-house.

"Uncle Matt!" Callie ran to him with her arms raised.

"Howdy, little Miz Heifer," he said. He set his cup on the table and lifted Callie to his hip and kissed her nose. "I've been a-waiting to see you."

"Pa, you stay and visit with Matt," Sarah said, walking toward the kitchen door. "I'll sit with Ma for a while."

"Where's Aunt Tillie?" Callie looked around the kitchen as if she thought Tillie was hiding from her.

"Alright, Sarah," Thurston said. "We'll be in directly. She's been asking for Matt."

"She had to stay at home this morning, sugar," Matt said. "But maybe you can come see us real soon."

Thurston looked at the fine lines at the corners of Matt's eyes as he talked to Callie. *Too harsh. Shouldn't have said what I said. He's like my own blood, my own son. My brother in Christ…*

"How's Retty doing, Thurston?" he said and sat Callie in a chair. They shook hands and Matt looked him straight in the eye.

"Not well a-tall, I'm afraid, Matt," he said.

"Ma's bad sick," Callie said.

"Well, we're just gonna have to pray for our acceptance of the Lord's will, little Heifer," Matt said.

"How's Tillie doing?" Thurston said.

"She's just fine," Matt said, thinking, *He don't know any more than me*. "She wishes there was something she could do to help out."

"No, no, Matt," he said. "You tell her we all unnerstand her condition and for her to take care of herself."

"We sent word by Luke yesterday that we got plenny room at our house for any of the folks to stay," he said. "And this morning, Tillie told me to be sure and bring Martha and Seth up there. Course, she's wanting to love on this little feller." Matt touched Nathan's cheek then picked up his coffee cup.

"We're obliged for y'all's help, Matt."

"You know I'd do anything for Retty and you, too, Thurston. We're grateful that we can help and expect some of the folks to come stay with us."

"We're looking for Morgan and Amanda and Erin and Richard to come in anytime now," Thurston said. "We'll make some kind of arrangements then, if that's alright by you."

"Ain't no hurry, Thurston," he said and sipped his bitter, black draught.

Chapter Twenty-five

Luke stood on the front porch with Horace and Ben Odom and Sidney and Joe and Walter Burgess. Ben and Walter stood uneasily apart from the men. At Asa's ma's insistence, Ben and William and Asa had made friends with Walter during Elder Purdy's summer writing school the first two weeks in July after the cotton crops were laid by. Since Asa bloodied his nose, Walter had been quiet, almost invisible at the spring during church singing, and Asa told Ben and William that sometimes Joe Burgess brought Walter with him when he came to court Maud.

Richard Hemphill stepped out of the house onto the porch and quietly shut the door behind him.

"I think I was the last one here to cross the Buskin Bridge this morning," Richard said. "It don't look like much of a rise on the creek to me."

"It didn't rain real hard at my place but once, about ten o'clock last night," Sidney said. "Now, it came down by the bucketsful then but since it's just been a slack rain."

"Yeah, but that first hard rain was hard enough to knock the cotton outta the hulls," Harvey said.

Richard pulled his pipe and a kitchen match from his coat pocket. He burst the match head with his thumbnail, and cupping the fire with his hands, he puffed the pipe to life.

"That pipe sure smells good, Uncle Richard," Luke said. He watched the road expecting to see Seth returning from his chores at any moment.

"It tastes good," Richard said. "And it relaxes a feller too. You oughta give it a try."

"I did once. Made me sick as a dog."

"Yeah, sometimes things are better smelling than tasting," Richard said and blew a stream of smoke through his nostrils.

"That's a certainty." Luke nodded his head.

"I see a wagon a-coming up the road, Luke," Joe said.

"That's Uncle Morgan, but I'm looking for Seth to get back purty soon, too. I'll open the gate for them," Luke said and walked down the porch steps.

"Looks like he's got him a covered wagon," Richard said.

To keep them all out of the rain, Morgan had draped an oilskin canvas over hickory standards nailed at the four corners of the wagon. The rain had stopped, but the sky gave no sign of clearing, and the air was cool and muggy. Morgan and Amanda rode on the wagon seat, and William and Asa sat behind them on a plank laid between the sideboards. William held their blowgun and the hickory reaming rod in his hand.

Morgan halted the mules at the front gate and wrapped the reins round a seat stanchion.

"Amanda, you and the boys unload here," he said climbing down the front wheel spokes. "I'll drive the wagon round to the barn and unhitch."

Amanda slid across the seat, stepped out on a front wheel spoke, and Morgan held her by the waist as she climbed down from the wagon. Asa and William jumped from the tailgate of the wagon to the muddy ground.

"You boys are just trying to get muddy!" Amanda said as they ran to the front gate. "And don't be running and jumping with them sticks in your hands, William."

"It's a blowgun, Ma," he said over his shoulder.

Luke held the gate open.

"You boys slow down," he said as Asa and William ran to the porch. "Good morning, Aunt Amanda."

"Good morning, Luke," she said and hugged him. "How's your ma?"

"Not doin' well," he said and shook his head.

"We're making a blowgun, Ben!" William said. "You and Walter can help us!"

"William," Amanda said. "Don't be so loud, son. Your Aunt Retty's sick."

"Howdy, Amanda," Horace said and shook her hand.

"Howdy, Horace," she said and turned to Richard. "Are your boys here, Richard?" She hugged his neck.

"No, we sent 'em to Clemson to let Hannah and Lee know that Retty's sick and cautioned 'em that the house better still be setting on blocks when we get back home this evening," he said and chuckled.

"Why, Richard Hemphill, them boys are about the best-behaved boys on the Hennessey," she said. "Why, it ain't been two days since I told Morgan that if William acted half as mannered as y'all's boys do, I'd never have to raise my voice."

"Thank you, Amanda," he said and opened the door for her.

She went into the big front room followed by Asa, William, Ben and Walter. Erin and Matt and Elder Purdy rose from their chairs to meet them. Martha kept her seat in a rocking chair holding Nathan.

"How's Retty? Did she get easy?" Amanda said. She and Erin embraced.

"She's sleeping a lot," Erin said. She had brown eyes and black hair streaked with gray. "But that potion of laudanum old Doc Foley gave her addled her so that you can't tell if she's easy or just can't say if she's hurting or not." She touched her fingertips to her sunken right cheek.

"Let's just hope and pray she's resting easy," Amanda said, and turning, she hugged Matt.

"Did y'all get rained on?" he asked.

“It came a shower just as we left Grandma’s,” she said. “But it slacked off and quit before we got to the Buskin Road bridge.”

“Is there much rise on the creek?” Matt asked.

“I couldn’t tell if there was any,” Amanda said.

“I guess we’re in for a spell of weather,” he said. “Like most folks here abouts, I’ve got a goodly portion of my crop left in the field.”

“How’s Tillie faring?” she asked.

“She’s just fine, Amanda. getting anxious.”

“Howdy, Sister Knox,” Elder Purdy said. He took her hand in both of his.

“I’m well, Elder Purdy,” she said. “How’s your folks?”

“Right well, thank the Lord.”

“I’ve gotta have a little of Nathan’s sugar this morning,” she said, and bending, she kissed his plump cheek. “Where’s Seth?”

“He went home to feed and milk,” Martha said. “He oughta be back directly.”

As the grown folks talked, William and Ben and Walter followed Asa as he edged around the room to where Thurston and Sarah sat at the bedside. Asa stood at Sarah’s elbow and watched his ma’s labored breathing. Her eyes were closed, and small red spots dotted her cheeks.

“Brother Thurston, don’t get up,” Elder Purdy said and offered his hand. “I’m a-needing to head on back to the house while this rain is slacked, but me and Effie will be back sometimes in the early afternoon.”

“We’re obliged, Elder Purdy,” he said and shook hands with the preacher.

“I’ll go out and give you a hand hitching up, Elder Purdy,” Matt said. “I’m needing to get back home and see how Tillie’s faring and catch up on my chores.”

“I’d appreciate it, Brother Matt.”

"I'll be back this afternoon, Thurston," Matt said and laid his hand on his shoulder.

Thurston pressed his hand and nodded. "You see to Tillie first."

"Morgan's at the barn unhitching our wagon by now," Amanda said. "He'll give y'all a hand."

"I'll take all the help I can git, Sister Amanda," Elder Purdy said, and he went out the back door ahead of the young deacon.

"Sarah," Asa whispered. "Is Ma a-sleeping?"

*

Matt latched the lot gate.

"Come up, mules," Elder Purdy said, and chucked at the mules and slapped the reins over their backs. As the wagon lumbered into the mire of the Buskin Road, Matt walked back into the barn.

"What I wanna ask you, Morgan," Matt said, "is if maybe you and Amanda and William might wanna come up to our place to spend the night. It ain't that far, and there ain't hardly room for ever'body down here." He picked up a corncob from the dusty barn floor, leaned against a post at the milking stall for balance, and scraped muddy dung from his shoe soles.

"That's so," Morgan said. "But I'd hate to go off and leave Thurston with Retty the shape she's in. He might be in need of help before morning."

"That's a fact," Matt said. He straightened from the post and tossed the muddied corncob out the barn door. "Do you suppose you could let Amanda and William go?"

"Amanda might be willing," he said.

"Seth told Martha for her to be the judge about going," Matt said. "And I figure she'd be more of a mind to go if Amanda was to go, too."

"I'll ask her about it after while, let her feel like she's been of some help, then I'll approach her. She might be willing to go."

"That'll be fine," Matt said. "I need to go home, now and see about Tillie, so y'all have plenny of time to talk it over."

"I'll help you saddle."

"Naw, you go on up to the house, Morgan. I'm of a mind that Thurston is wanting you with him."

*

By late morning, the big front room and porch and kitchen-house were crowded with friends and family. Fresh baked corn bread, biscuits, fried chicken and ham covered the kitchen shelf and most of the table. At one end of the table, Asa and Walter carded raw cotton that Sarah had given them to fletch their blowgun arrows, and William and Ben used butcher knives to carefully split ten-inch splinters from a block of straight grained pine that Luke had picked out for them. William laid a splinter beside the two on the table they'd already cut from the block. Later, they would shave and rub them to just the right taper and smoothness for arrow shafts, burn the tips to harden them, and twist cotton fluff around the thicker end for fletching.

Seth and Luke and Sidney and Joe Burgess stood on the front porch near the door to the big front room.

"It appears like this rain ain't gonna let up," Seth said in a lowered voice.

"I don't recall the weather ever being this poorly at picking time," Sidney murmured and shook his head.

In the front room, Erin sat beside Richard next to the fireplace. She and Bertie Odom, Fleeta Burgess and Gertrude Jurgens occasionally spoke in hushed voices. Thurston and Maud sat at Retty's bedside. Retty breathed with quick, shallow breaths as Maud gently wiped her face with a damp flannel cloth. On the other side of the bed, Morgan sat with his head in his hands, and Amanda stood behind him, one hand resting on his shoulder.

Erin looked past the window curtains and saw a rider wearing a black slicker and felt hat on a gray horse plodding up the road, a specter in the mist of rain. A feeling of dread sank through her bowels, and she touched her sunken cheek.

When she was six years old, she came down with a bad stomachache, and her pa rode his horse over and fetched Doc Foley. He came with his black pill bag full of potions and dosed her with a dime's worth of calomel. That evening, she got sick to her stomach, and slobber poured from her mouth like warm, salty grease. She gulped until she could swallow no more.

"Oh, my heavens, George!" her ma said. "This child is salivating. Bring me a basin." But she vomited before her pa got the basin to her bedside. And she came down with such a bad case of dysentery that her ma put her in napkins like an infant, and her pa made a cot of poles and bed ticking for her that could be easily stripped, and changed fresh every day. Within a week, the inside of her mouth became raw and lined with pus, and the flesh died and sloughed off in strips and chunks. Her teeth loosened, and she spat them out with bloody pus and sloughed flesh into the washbasin her ma held for her. She prayed for God to take her. He didn't, and she slowly recovered, almost toothless. In a couple of years, she got her permanent teeth, but her right cheek was paper thin and had grown to her gums, forever sunken. She feared Dr. Foley, who rode through the mist of her dim, childhood memories.

"Doc Foley just rode up," Erin said. "Guess it's 'bout time for us to go get a sip of coffee, ain't it, Richard?"

"Yeah," he said. He nodded at the mantle clock. "It's nigh on to eleven o'clock, and I wanna smoke my pipe, too."

"I guess we oughta start stirring up something for folks to eat," Bertie said.

Fleeta nodded at Gertrude, and they stood.

"We'll help you stir, Bertie," Gertrude said.

The front and back doors of the kitchen-house stood open. The stove still held live coals, and in spite of the rain, the air in the kitchen was overly warm. The four boys sat at the table making their blowgun arrows.

Erin chuckled as she and Richard and Bertie crossed the walk to the kitchen-house.

"What's goosed you?" Richard said.

"It just come to mind the time Thurston fell off the kitchen-house walk when we was young'uns, and Pa's old hounds like to have ate him alive."

"I've heard your ma tell that tale," Richard said. He smiled as they entered the kitchen. "Y'all about got that blowgun made, boys?"

"Yes sir," Asa said. "We're making arrows now."

"What happened to Mr. Thurston and the hounds, Miz Erin?" Walter asked.

"Well, Walter, our pa always throwed the table scraps off the walk between the kitchen-house and the main house for his ole hounds, and one evening after supper, Ma stuck a finger-hole in a biscuit and poured surp in it for Thurston. He jumped up from the table with his biscuit to run back into the house. It was raining just about like now, but it was in January, not long after Christmas, and it was cold." She lifted the coffeepot and shook it. "Don't you figure I may as well make a fresh pot, Richard?"

"I'd say so. I suspect there's plenny folks here to help drink it," he said. He picked up one of the boys' pine splinters. "Here boys, let me harden one of your arrow tips for you." He leaned forward in his chair and opened the firebox and held the splinter in the coals until it burst into flame. Sitting back, he cupped the fire over the bowl of his pipe.

"Thurston musta been about eight or nine years old," Erin said. "I was six or seven."

She walked to the china safe, talking over her shoulder as she got down the coffee grinder and set it on the table.

"Here, Erin," Bertie said. "I brought a small sack of coffee beans that I parched last night. Let's use them first."

"Thank you, Bertie," she said and took the sack of beans. "About the time he hit the middle of the walk, his feet slipped from under him on the wet boards." She poured the coffee beans into the grinder. "He squalled like a wildcat and fell to the ground. It's a thousand wonders the fall hadn't killed him, but it didn't." She ladled a dipper of water from the stove reservoir into the coffeepot. "Them dogs set in to growling and snarling and a-snapping. They must've thought Pa had throwed out more table scraps, and they was fightin over Thurston and his biscuit. About the time Thurston squalled, Pa come up outta his chair and ran out on the walk and jumped down amongst hounds, Thurston, and all and commenced to kicking and throwing dogs ever' which-a-way and pulled Thurston outta the fight." She sloshed the water around inside the coffeepot, walked to the back door and dashed the coffee dregs into the yard. "Pa laid him up on the walk, and the little feller's arms and legs was cut and bleeding, and blood run down his face from a coupla bites in his scalp, but he was still clutching half of that biscuit in his fist."

Erin chuckled as she began to turn the handle on the grinder. The aroma of freshly ground coffee flooded the kitchen-house.

"Alright, boys," Bertie said. "Y'all take your blowgun makings out to the barn, and we'll call y'all to dinner after the grown-ups finish eating."

Chapter Twenty-six

After they raked the scraps into the yard for the hounds and carried their plates and forks into the kitchen, the men loitered on the back porch talking in low murmurs. A fine mist hung like a veil between the house and woods, and water dripped from the eaves. Seth and Luke stood near the edge of the porch.

"How long has he been in there, now?" Luke said.

Sidney Burgess held his watch by a leather fob and said, "I'd say nigh on to two hours."

"When he came out for a bite to eat, I askt him if there was no hope, and he said, 'Yeah, God's own mercy,'" Seth said. He leaned with one hand high on a porch post, spat tobacco juice into the rain puddled yard and lowered his head.

Richard pulled his pipe and tobacco pouch from his coat pocket and squatted with his back to the wall.

"They say in his day, old Doc Foley kept plenny of folks alive on the Hennessey," he said, and with his forefinger, he tamped tobacco into the bowl of his pipe. "But Erin's scared to death of him." He struck a match on his thumbnail and puffed the pipe to life.

"It looks like it's gonna come another shower," Seth said as the rain spattered louder on the roof. "I hope Matt made it to his place without gittin' rained on."

"He said he was gonna see after Tillie and do his chores then come on back," Richard said. "That Matt's a fine young feller."

"Me and him and Luke grew up like brothers," Seth said.

The dripping rain became a steady stream from the eaves.

*

Quietly, Joe Burgess sat at one end of the crowded kitchen table and watched Maud as she dipped hot water from the stove reservoir into a dishpan.

"You boys finish eating and get outta the kitchen," Maud said. "We've gotta clean up in here."

"Our blowgun stuff is out in the barn," William said.

"I wanna make a blowgun, too," Callie said.

"Well, y'all get on out there before it sets in to raining again," Amanda said and stacked dishes on the kitchen shelf.

"Me and Maud need you to help us, Callie," Sarah said.

The boys pushed from the table and crowded through the door. Walter following grabbed the last biscuit from the platter.

"Walter, ain't you had enough to eat, son," Fleeta said.

"Let that boy get plenny to eat, Fleeta," Bertie said. "He's still growing."

"Which means he needs to learn his manners," Fleeta said.

"Did anybody let Hannah know that Retty's sick?" Gertrude asked.

"Yeah," Erin said. "Richard sent our boys to Clemson to let her and Lee know."

"Maud, why don't you and Sarah go in and sit with your ma and the other folks?" Gertrude said. "We'll clean up in here."

"Ma's bad sick," Callie said.

"No, I think Aunt Erin oughta go," Maud said and nodded at Callie. "We took Callie in earlier and now she's gonna help us in the kitchen."

"Well, I don't relish Doc Foley's company," Erin said. "But I guess I oughta be there."

*

Wake and sleep had become as one for Retty.

The doors were open for the spring breeze to freshen the house.

"I hoped for better for my girls, Rufe," her ma said. "I just can't help it. He's nothing."

"What's wrong, Ma?" Retty said.

"He's nothing, Retty," she said. "You'll never have anything married to the likes of him."

"Thurston Knox is a decent young feller," her pa said.

"Matt's my son, Ma."

"And Tillie's your daughter-in-law!"

"It breaks my heart, Ma. All of it! All of it breaks my heart!"

"Now you know!"

Retty gasped for breath.

So hard to breath.

"I just can't do it, Rufe," her ma said.

"Feel, Retty," Tillie said.

She pressed Retty's hand to her warm, swollen belly. Retty pulled her hand away, surprised and ill at ease that she had touched her in such an intimate way.

"On my side, Retty," she said. "Your grandchild. Feel her kick." She smiled and pulled Retty's hand to her side. "Our first. We're gonna name her Retty."

Her feet grew numb with cold.

And the sun climbed, bright for all the world, and she felt light, free, and a great weight lifted from her. She almost laughed for the joy of it. The bright sun, not a summer bright that made a fellow squint from sunup till sundown, but a spring bright that showed up everything sharp and clean all at once like the whole world was one big eye, and her pa drove the wagon, and Hannah sat on the seat between him and her ma, and she and Thurston sat in chairs behind, everyone dressed in their Sunday best. Her ma turned and smiled at her.

*

Beside the fireplace, Erin slowly rocked and read her Bible. Thurston sat at Retty's bedside and held her hand in both of his. Dr. Foley stood beside Thurston, his stethoscope hanging from his neck. He cleared his throat and ambled across the room and peered through the front window and ran the knuckle of his forefinger under his moustache. The mantle clock struck three, and he drew his watch from his vest pocket with a gold fob, glanced at it, and returned it to his pocket. He walked back and stood next to Thurston. Morgan sat on the opposite side of the bed and silently prayed without ceasing. Amanda stood behind him with her head bowed and a hand on his shoulder. Rain tapping on the board shingles muted the distant clack and scrape of chinaware being washed and stacked away in the kitchen-house. A faint whiff of Richard's pipe tobacco winnowed into the room. The mantle clock ticked.

My honey, my love, my heart's above.

Thurston looked down at Retty, her pale skin blotched with red spots, her breathing labored.

"The purtiest girl from Nashobee Lake to Hennessey Creek," Horace Odom had said, and he was right.

Wordlessly, she opened her eyes, and he felt himself drawn into the blueness. She sighed, a long sigh that ended with a rattle.

Thurston sat back in his chair, holding her hand. Dr. Foley waited for her to draw another breath.

Erin glanced up from her reading and saw Thurston's face.

She rocked forward and stood, laid her Bible in the seat of the rocking chair and stepped to the foot of the bed.

Dr. Foley leaned over the bed and pressed the cone of his stethoscope to her chest for a long moment.

"God's will be done." He gently closed her eyes with a downward draw of his thumb and forefinger.

Thurston nodded his head.

"Oh, Retty!" Erin rushed to Thurston's side and wrapped her arms around his shoulders.

On the porch, they heard Erin's voice and looked at each other in silent dread. Richard knocked his pipe into his palm and tossed the fiery dottle into the yard. It hissed and died in the puddled rain. Reluctantly, they shuffled through the door into the big front room.

Chapter Twenty-seven

Dr. Foley folded his stethoscope into his bag, stood and with the bag bumping his leg, he walked to the front window. He looked across the porch into the cotton field and waited. He needed to talk to Gertrude and the two ladies that would be helping her. He knew that Gertrude often led or helped in the laying out of deceased friends and neighbors, but he wanted to make sure that she and the other ladies understood the need for haste in laying out Retty's corpse.

Thurston glanced up and saw Dr. Foley at the window. He stood and said, "Folks, let's go on over to the kitchen-house and have coffee and leave the room for Gertrude and the ladies." Heads nodded.

Gertrude tugged Frank's arm and whispered in his ear. He cut his eyes at Dr. Foley, patted her hand and followed the crowd out of the room. Gertrude, Bertie and Fleeta walked to where the doctor waited.

"Ladies," he said. "I know all of you have experience in laying out the deceased, but this may be a first for y'all. Retty's body is full of blood poison. So, to speak frankly, decomposition is going to set in quicker than usual, and y'all will be getting the odor in twenty-four hours if not sooner. You'll need to cool the corpse as quick as you can. I suggest you leave all windows and outside doors open and that you wash her body with fresh cold well water and camphor for three or four hours and longer if necessary to lower her temperature as quick as possible."

A knock and the back porch door opened, and Horace Odom leaned into the room.

"Sorry, Doc. Take all the time y'all need. I just wanna let you know that I'm a-waiting out here to give you a hand saddling up when you get ready to leave, but no hurry."

"I'm obliged, Horace. I'll be there directly," he said and nodded and turned to Gertrude. "I suspect it would be best to not wait for the cooling board and go ahead and flush her bowels and bladder and start washing her down. If you have to hold her on a bedpan on the bed, why go ahead. That feather bed will have to be burnt anyhow on account of the seepage from her leg."

"I figure we can have her ready by the time we get the coffin," Gertrude said.

"I hope with the cold water washing that the rigors will pass in less than twenty hours. I have seen cases when the corpse went through very little or no rigor mortis," Dr. Foley said. "Anyhow, y'all should wash her three or four hours with cold water and camphor to cool her off as fast as you can, and that'll help keep the odor down, too."

*

The smell of dank hay and livestock stomp hung in the barn hall. The boys gathered in the light of the open door and with pieces of broken glass carefully scraped their pine splinters into smooth and tapered blowgun arrows.

"Y'all think a feller could kill a squirrel with one of these arrows?" Walter said.

"Sure nuff," William said.

"Seth and Luke and Uncle Matt kilt rabbits with theirs," Asa said.

The barn door opened, and the boys looked up from their work.

"Asa, you boys c'mon to the kitchen-house," Luke said. "Pa wants to talk to ever'body."

The boys hurriedly piled their arrows and broken glass under the saddle pole in the corner of the barn. Luke stood by the gate to shut and latch it. Asa looked up at him when he went out, but Luke didn't look at him. Asa knew something was bad wrong, and his heart began to pound.

Luke followed the boys, and Dr. Foley and Horace Odom walked down the back porch steps.

"I'm gonna give Doc Foley a hand saddling up, Luke. I'll be back in directly."

"C'mon in when you're done, Mr. Odom," Luke said. "We're much obliged, Dr. Foley."

"God bless you, son," Dr. Foley said.

Luke climbed the steps behind the boys into the kitchen and stood in the doorway.

Thurston sat at the table with his back to the wall. Callie curled in his lap, her face buried in his bosom. His eyes and nose were red, and he clutched a crumpled handkerchief in his hand. He sat straight in his chair and held his head up. Sarah leaned at his shoulder, and Maud stood at his other side and clutched a handkerchief in her hands and bowed her head. Joe stood beside her with his arm around her waist. Across the table, Martha held Nathan and Seth stood behind her, and Erin and Amanda sat side by side next to Martha. Richard stood behind Erin. Asa slipped behind Morgan who sat at the end of the table and stood in front of Sarah beside his pa. William and Ben stopped beside Morgan, and Walter edged to Joe's side.

"Young'uns, your ma's gone," Thurston said in a steady, strong voice. "Dr. Foley and all of us did ever'thing we humanly could and knew how to do, but she was just too tired and too sick." His voice quivered, then. "All her pain's over now, and she's at peace with the Lord, and we've got to go on."

Asa had never heard his pa's voice sound like that. He remembered how he'd cussed him in his head because he whipped him for fighting Walter at church. His shoulders trembled, and his breath came in jerks. Tears ran down his cheeks, and he hid his eyes in the crook of his arm and sobbed. He would never again run into the warm kitchen on a cold morning and see her standing at the cookstove, the smell of bacon and biscuits. He would never again hear her voice call him into the house at dusk. She was gone.

"I know y'all loved your ma, and she loved y'all. If y'all feel like she may've done wrong by you sometimes, forgive her. She was trying to do the best she knew to be a good ma." Maud sobbed into her handkerchief. "And if you feel like you may've done her wrong, forget about that too, because she forgave you a long time ago. She loved and respected her sisters and brothers, whether natural or married in. She loved God, her church and her brothers and sisters in Christ. We're all gonna sorely miss her. God's will be done." He pressed his handkerchief to his eyes, his shoulders shaking.

Asa had never seen his pa cry. He edged closer to his pa, and his pa slipped an arm round his shoulders and hugged him.

"It's alright, son. It's alright." He patted Asa's shoulder then rubbed his hand through his hair, and he said again, "It's alright." Finally, he sat up straight and blew his nose. "I hate it young'uns, but we're gonna have to bury your ma tomorrow as soon as we can. Dr. Foley said as bad as the poison is in her blood, we shouldn't wait, so Luke, I want you to hitch up the wagon, and Richard, if you would, I want you to go with Luke, and y'all drive into Clemson and buy a coffin. It's almost three o'clock now, so you probably won't get there before Hunter's Mercantile closes for the night. Y'all can stay at Hannah and Lee's place. Luke, they'll wanna know that your ma has passed away and tell them the reason we have to bury her in such a hurry tomorrow. I have credit at Hunter's for next year's cotton seed, so get a nice coffin with brass fittings."

"Should they get a shroud, too, Thurston?" Erin asked.

"No, Erin, Retty wants her Sunday frock."

"Do you want us to go by and let Grandma and Grandpa know?" Luke asked.

"No, son," he said. "Y'all go directly to town. Doc Foley's gonna stop by to see them on his way home, and I asked him to tell 'em not to set out this late in this weather. Morgan'll bring'em over in the morning."

"Pa, don't you suspect Mr. Odom can make as good a coffin as you can buy?" Seth said.

"I figure he can, Seth, but your ma's folks is all proper buried in store-bought coffins, and she's gonna be too."

The room became silent.

"After y'all get hitched up, Luke," Seth said, "bring me the hammer an' screwdriver from the toolbox.".

Luke looked at him as though he hadn't understood him.

"We're gonna have to take down one of the doors for a cooling board."

Luke nodded.

Richard clamped his pipe bit between his teeth and followed Luke out the kitchen-house door.

"Seth," Thurston said. "Go to the smokehouse, son, and bring in a ham, and Sarah, stir up the fire in the stove and get the old black pot to boil the ham in. Folks will bring more food stuff tomorrow but we gotta have something to eat till then."

"Yes sir," Sarah said.

"Asa, you boys go draw a bucket of water and set it on the back porch for Miz Jurgens and then fetch a bucket for Sarah to boil the ham. After y'all get that done, y'all can go work on your blowgun if you feel like it."

"Yes sir, Pa," Asa said.

As the table cleared, Thurston leaned back, wiped his palm over his mustache and sighed.

"You want me to hold Callie and let you lie down for a spell, Pa?" Maud said.

"No. Just let me sit here and rest," he said. "But if you would, get your ma's Sunday frock outta the chifforobe and your sewing basket for Gertrude and the ladies." As Maud went out the door he said, "And lay out a couple of old sheets for Horace and Frank and a couple of your ma's old nightgowns for Gertrude and the ladies. They'll make washrags. When you come back, you can hold Callie awhile."

"Doc Foley is on his way home," Horace said. As he came in the backdoor, he patted Seth's shoulder. "Luke gave me the screwdriver and hammer." Seth nodded.

"Can I give y'all a hand, Sarah?" Amanda said and stood from her chair.

"You could pick us out about a dozen sweet potatoes from the potato box, Aunt Amanda," Sarah said. "We need to cook up a little something to go with the ham for folks to eat this evening."

"I'll hold Callie now, Pa," Maud said as she walked back into the kitchen. "You sit with me and Joe, Callie." Callie reached her arms up, and Maud lifted her from Thurston's lap.

Horace laid the screwdriver and hammer on the table and sat beside Frank facing Thurston across the table. Joe sat on a chair against the kitchen wall, and Maud sat on the chair next to him with Callie nestled at her bosom.

Seth stepped through the backdoor and handed Sarah the ham and the bucket of water that Asa had drawn from the well.

"I see Matt coming, now," Seth said. "I'm gonna go help him with his horse."

"Break the news to him, son," Thurston said and rested his hands on the table. "He dearly loved your ma."

Seth nodded and stepped out the backdoor and met Asa.

"Uncle Matt's coming," Asa said. He had drawn the second bucket of water.

"I see him," Seth said. "Let me have the bucket of water, and I'll set it on the porch. You go and open the lot gate for Matt, and y'all can work on your blowgun and arrows. I'll be there directly to help Matt with his horse."

*

Horace watched as Thurston slowly traced the tip of his forefinger along the pale, fishhook-shaped scar that curved around his knuckle and shanked in the fleshy web between his thumb and forefinger. When it happened, he and Thurston were sitting on the top rail of the split-rail fence peeling and chewing sugarcane. Across the yard, smoke lazily rose from under his pa's sugar kettle and faded into the sunny, fall sky, and Thurston's knife blade slipped on the hard, smooth sugarcane peel and sliced into his hand.

Lord! Thurston dropped his knife and grabbed his hand. By the time Horace helped him climb down from the fence, his hand was bleeding like a stuck pig, and he led him to where the men fed cane into the mill. All the while, Thurston held the cut closed, trying to staunch the bleeding. Thurston's pa wrapped a rag around his hand, and it just soaked up the blood, and Mr. George looked at Horace's pa and said, "Hugh, you gonna have to ride over to my place and tell Onie that Thurston cut his hand and we can't stop the bleeding." And his pa unhitched one of the mules from the cane mill, swung up on his back, and took off at a swooping gallop, his elbows flapping. He was gone just about long enough to get to the Knox's place when Thurston's hand stopped bleeding. Horace's pa later said he told Miss Onie what had happened and that she nodded her head, reached down her Bible from the mantelpiece and opened it. He said she sort of turned her back to him and he didn't see which passage she read from, and she commenced to pray. Just mumbling and groaning like, and directly, she turned, looked up and smiled at him and said, "The

Lord's will be done, Hugh, and you tell George Knox to keep an eye on that boy." And when the bleeding stopped, it stopped cold. Thurston's pa unwrapped his hand, and the cut opened like where you'd cut a hog's throat, all raw, red meat, but not a drop of blood ran from the gash.

Miz Onie Knox is a sure nuff strange woman.

*

"Frank, y'all can come set up the cooling board, now," Gertrude said.

They looked up at Gertrude standing at the kitchen door. The faint odor of camphor drifted into the room. Horace and Sidney rose from their chairs, and Frank stood holding the hammer and screwdriver.

"I'll give y'all a hand with the cooling board, Horace," Sidney said.

"Erin, give me two cups of coffee, please ma'am," Gertrude said.

"No need, Sidney," Horace said. "Me and Frank'll take care of it. You stay here and visit with the folks."

"Sugar and cream?" Erin asked.

With a faint clacking of china, Sarah set out two cups and saucers on the table.

"Just coffee," Gertrude said.

Erin poured the coffee.

"Thank you, honey," Gertrude said. She took one cup and saucer from Sarah, and Horace took the other.

"Y'all can use the door to the boys' room, Horace," Thurston said.

Horace nodded, and he and Frank followed Gertrude across the walk and the back porch. Stepping through the open door into the front room, the two men stood in the cool silence of camphor. Bertie sat in a chair next to the bed where Retty's corpse lay covered with a sheet, and Fleeta stood at the foot of the bed.

"Fleeta, while Horace and Frank get started setting up the cooling board, you and Bertie drank your coffee," Gertrude said and handed Fleeta the coffee.

"Coffee would go good about now," Fleeta said.

"Horace, Maud laid out a couple old sheets and a quilt on the vanity that y'all can use." Bertie put the flannel washrag she had been using in a basin on the bedside table and rose from her chair. "I could use a stretch of my limbs and a sip of coffee." She took the cup and saucer from Horace.

"That's the door Thurston said to use," Horace said and nodded at the door that led into the boys' bedroom. "Have you got the hammer and screwdriver?"

"Yeah," Frank said. "I got 'em."

Horace opened the door and held it, and Frank knelt on the floor and with the hammer and screwdriver, tapped the pin out of the bottom hinge and stood and tapped the pin out of the top hinge. Together, they carried the door across the room and stood it on the hinge-edge in front of the cold fireplace. With the door leaned against his legs, Frank used the screwdriver to remove the door latch and knobs while Horace set two straight chairs for stands. Neither spoke. When all was readied, they laid the door between the chairs each end on the seats of the two straight chairs making a low, narrow table.

"Where's them old sheets and quilt, Bertie?" Horace asked.

"They're on top of the vanity."

"Here," Frank said. "I'll get 'em."

He reached the quilt and sheets and handed a sheet to Horace. Horace shook out the sheet and spread it over the door and they tucked the ends between the chair seats and the door. Frank folded the quilt into a pillow and set it at one end of the door. Horace ripped the other sheet in two and handed half of it to Frank. They tore the sheet into strips and laid the strips across the cooling board.

"I guess we done about all we can do," Frank said and nodded at Gertrude.

"Set another bucket of fresh well water on the back porch, Frank," Gertrude said. "And we'll throw this feather bedding out in the front yard directly for y'all to burn. We'll let y'all know when we're done in here, but it's gonna be sometime into the night."

Frank nodded and walked out the door.

*

"Y'all want coffee?" Erin asked.

"I don't think I do, Erin," Horace said, and Frank shook his head.

"Howdy, Matt," Frank said as he and Horace sat down at the kitchen table.

"Howdy, Frank, Horace," Matt said and nodded at each man in turn. His eyes were red-rimmed.

"I'm afraid you've come back to sad news," Frank said.

"It wa'n't unexpected," Matt said.

"I hope you didn't get rained on going and coming," Horace said.

"Naw, I made the trip between showers," Matt said. "Looks like it's trying to clear up and it's starting to turn cooler. I'd venture to say, ain't nobody gonna make much cotton this year even if the rain stops now."

"Another day or two of this rain and it'll rot in the bolls," Sidney said.

"That's a fact," Horace said.

"Thurston, I hate it, but we're gonna have to burn Retty's feather bed," Frank said. "Where do you want us to build the fire?"

"I knew it was gonna have to be burnt," he said. "We got all our corn in, so anywhere around the cornfield will be likely. That's far enough from the house we ought not get too much burnt feather smell from it."

Chapter Twenty-eight

"Get them tie-downs outta the way there, Gertrude, and we'll move her onto the cooling board," Fleeta said. "Frank and Horace made a fine cooling board. I'd like to have a pillow, folded quilt or otherwise, under my head, too. I hope somebody does as well for me."

"I'm of a mind your corpse ain't gonna care one way or the other," Gertrude said and smiled at Bertie.

"I know my corpse ain't gonna care, then," Fleeta said. "But I'm a-caring right now."

"Alright, Fleeta," Bertie said. "We'll see to it for you. Now, watch her head when you lift. It's gonna flop back."

"I got it," she said.

Leaving the covering sheet in place over the corpse, Fleeta slipped her hands under her armpits and lifted, her head resting against her belly, and Gertrude gripped her ankles and lifted. Bertie rolled the feather bedding into a tight bundle as Fleeta and Gertrude shuffled across the room and stretched Retty's corpse on the cooling board resting her head on the folded quilt.

"She ain't very heavy," Fleeta said, thinking, *This is the other grandma of my coming grand-young'uns.* She stepped back and pulled her handkerchief from her pocket and wiped her eyes.

"Open the door for me, Gertrude," Bertie said, "and I'll throw this bedding out for Frank to burn."

"Let me help you carry it."

"No. I got it in a good and tight bundle. You just open the door."

"I'll get the basin with fresh cold water and camphor, and we can get started washing and cooling her down," Fleeta said.

"She's not much heavier than a feather pillow," Gertrude said as she sat on a chair at Retty's head with her back to the cold fireplace.

"I'll venture, her ma, Miz Rachel Tarroll weighted as much as a small mule," Bertie said walking back into the room. "Should I leave this door open?" She sat on a chair next to Gertrude at Retty's legs.

"Yeah, we need all the cooling we can git," Gertrude said and turned down the sheet from over the corpse.

Fleeta brought the flannel rags in the wash basin and set the basin at the foot of the cooling board. They each took a rag and wrung it over the basin and Fleeta stood at Retty's head facing Gertrude. They began to wipe the corpse.

"That's a fact. Miz Rachel was might near big as me," Gertrude said and chuckled and gently wiped Retty's left shoulder and arm. "Did you ever know her, Fleeta? She was Retty's ma."

"No." she said. "I grew up over at Salem and didn't move out here until after me and Sid married. Of course, Sid knew them all, so I've known of her, who she was, but I never really was around her folks," she said.

"Gertrude's like me," Bertie said. "We knowed the Tarrolls all our lives."

"I guess so," Gertrude said. "Many's the time we danced in the Tarroll's parlor. As a matter of fact, Frank askt me to marry him at one of their play-parties."

"Horace talked Thurston into going to one of the parties," Bertie said. "And that might've been the first one Thurston ever went to because he said it was the first time he'd ever seen Retty. I think he'd seen her before, and just hadn't paid her no mind before that night. Anyhow, he kissed her right there on the dance floor, on the lips too." They laughed.

"I suspect that got ever'body's attention," Fleeta said and raised her eyebrows, smiling.

"It sure nuff did," Gertrude said. "Miz Rachel sat there frowning like a thunderstorm, but Mr. Rufe, he was a jovial sort of fellow, he just laughed and called Thurston a Hennessey Creek wild man or something like that."

"Well, when she died," Bertie said, "me and my ma and Ma's sister, my Aunt Ludie, laid her out. It was my first time ever helping with a laying out. Miz Rachel died of childbed fever after Matt was born. Retty and Thurston had been married about a year and had moved in with her folks after Matt was born and Miz Rachel got sick. She never got outta her bed after Matt was born. Well, Aunt Ludie's 'bout as thick as a match stem, and if you filled her pockets with rocks, she might balance a cotton scale at ninety pounds."

"Barely, I'd say." Gertrude said and chuckled. "If you'd soaked her in the creek for a couple hours."

"Anyhow," Bertie said. "We was standing there looking down at Miz Rachel's corpse laying on the bed, knowing we was faced with a hard chore gittin' it onto the cooling board, trying to figure out how the three of us was gonna manage, and Aunt Ludie says, 'Reckon we oughta get Retty in here to give us a hand.' And my ma spoke right up, 'No, Ludie,' she says. 'A body oughta have enough friends and neighbors to lay her out proper without her next of kin or strangers having to do it.' So, we did it. Heavy as a small mule, Miz Rachel was, but I always remembered what my ma said, and I'm of a mind she was right."

"And that's how Retty and Thurston ended up living with Mr. Rufe for over a year with Retty taking care of Matt like he was her own child," Gertrude said. "Matt's a little more than a year older than Seth and a couple of years older than Luke. They grew up like brothers."

"I guess Matt and Luke were heavy on her mind at the end," Fleeta said. "I overheard Maud telling Erin that Retty kept asking about them, and I wondered if there had been a row or something."

"Might be," Bertie said. "Y'all recall that Luke had a falling out with Thurston back in the winter and ran away from home, and Matt and Tillie took him in. Well, Horace met up with Matt down on the creek one day and said ever'thing seemed alright, but sudden like, Luke went back home."

"Well, I suppose ever'thing is settled now if there was a row," Fleeta said. "Matt was elected a deacon at Mount Olive in July and he and Tillie are expecting their first in December."

"Sounds settled to me," Gertrude said.

"I'll get the frock that Maud laid out for her and cut it down the back so it'll be ready to dress her as soon as we have her cooled down," Bertie said.

*

Thurston sat in silence and nodded his head.

"Thurston, I hate to bring it up," Matt said. "But we need to make some sleeping arrangements for tonight."

"Yeah, we do," Thurston said.

"Seth'll be comin' home with me for sure," Matt said. "And I figured on Callie and Asa coming too."

"Me and Bertie are goin' to set up tonight," Horace said. "And we'll have Ben. We were kinda counting on Asa being here."

"Ben can come with us," Matt said. "He'll be company for Asa."

"You sure it's alright," Horace said.

"Sure nuff," Matt said. "Morgan, you and Amanda come too. We got plenny room."

"We're obliged, Matt, but we figured on staying with Ma and Pa tonight," Morgan said.

"Well, let William come," Matt said. "Asa and Ben are gonna need all the help they can get making that blowgun."

"That's the truth," Amanda said and shook her head.

"We'll see," Morgan said.

"Frank, you and Sidney would do good to head out as quick as you can," Horace said. "The rain has let up, but them roads is apt to be mighty boggy."

"If y'all need more help diggin' the grave, my boys oughta be home sometimes this evening," Erin said.

"I figure me and Joe and Frank can get it done in plenny of time," Sidney said. "And me and Joe'll stop by your place, Horace, and feed and milk for you. You and Bertie don't worry 'bout nothing at home."

"I'll go do Horace's chores, Sidney," Frank said. "Gertrude is gonna stay here and set up tonight, too, so I can head out at any time, and I'll be riding alone."

"Horace's place is a mile beyond yours, Frank," Sidney said. "We'll go right past it on our way home."

"Naw, you oughta head directly home and get your folks outta this weather quick as you can," Frank said. "You'll need to rest up to help dig the grave in the morning."

"That may be best," Sidney said and nodded.

"I'm obliged, Frank," Horace said.

A sudden wind blew a chill through the kitchen-house, and the back door slammed shut.

"Looks like the weather's breaking," Thurston said.

"If you ever wondered why cemeteries are always on some hill or other," Frank said. "This weather sure tells the tale."

"Yeah," Thurston said and pensively, looking at nobody and nothing, he traced the fishhook-shaped scar that curved round his knuckle with the tip of his forefinger. "A rainy-day burying is a sure nuff hard chore."

*

They stood at their places on either side of the cooling board and Fleeta finished pinning Retty's hair in place and stepped back.

"How's that Gertrude: Did I get it right?"

"Not quite the same as she would've done it, Fleeta. What do you think, Bertie?" Gertrude stooped and straightened the collar of her Sunday frock.

"I'd say good enough for now. Maud or Erin can touch it up a mite after we get her laid out."

Bertie's voice ceased.

They shuffled their feet in the sudden quiet, uneasy at finding themselves standing so near such an awful, palpable certainty. Fleeta stared into the cold, dead fireplace thinking, *This is the other grandma of my grand-young'uns*. Looking at Retty's stripped bed, Gertrude felt a stir of dread in her bowels. The mantel clock ticked. Bertie looked through the raised front window. The slight odor of burnt feathers drifted in the darkness.

"Where's them tie-downs?" Bertie said. "We need to tie the corpse so it won't roll off the cooling board and will relax in place coming outta the rigors."

"I got 'em," Gertrude said, and handed strips to Fleeta and Bertie. "We got plenny o' time." She glanced at the mantle clock. "It'll be a couple more hours or so before her corpse is out of the rigors and we can bring the folks in, so let's not get in no hurry."

Gertrude wound a strip under Retty's chin, and knotting it on top of her head with a slip knot, she tied her mouth shut. Then, she overlapped Retty's hands on her stomach, left hand on top of her right, and said, "Tie one around here, Fleeta, while I hold her hands in place."

"I always wondered how come we place the left hand over the right," Bertie said. "It's mighty uncomfortable to me. Sometimes lying a-bed at night on my back, I put my left hand over my right jus' to try it out, but it's jus' not natural to me. I can't rest with my hands like that."

"I guess it's to show a lady's wedding band," Gertrude said.

"Ever'body knows I'm married, so don't worry about that when my time comes."

"Well, Bertie, when we lay you out, we'll put your right hand on top," Gertrude said and smiled. "And we'll put a pillow on Fleeta's cooling board. We'd want y'all resting easy."

"Here, take the end of this 'un," Fleeta said and stooped and handed the end of another tie-down under the cooling board to Bertie. Bertie pulled the tie under and handed it to Fleeta over the corpse. Fleeta slip-knotted it.

Gertrude placed a nickel on each of Retty's eyelids.

"How's it appear to y'all?" Fleeta said.

"I figure we got it," Bertie said.

"It appears her frock may be a little twisted," Gertrude said. "Strange that she asked Thurston to bury her in her Sunday frock and not in a shroud."

"You know, Retty was always thrifty. She wouldn't want to spend extra on no shroud," Bertie said. "We'll straighten out her clothes again when we lay her in the coffin."

"I thought maybe she wanted to be buried in her Sunday-go-to-church finery," Gertrude said.

"That's probably it," Fleeta said and wrung a camphor soaked cloth into the basin. "Here," she said, and turning to the head of the cooling board, she spread the flannel cloth over Retty's face. "I wisht we had some roses and cape jasmine."

"Flowers would be nice," Bertie said. "The camphor pretty much covers the odor, but…"

"Bless her heart," Gertrude said. "Before we call the folks in to sit, we'll go out in the yard and gather in some wax myrtle branches to scatter for her."

The End

Printed in the USA
CPSIA information can be obtained
at www.ICGtesting.com
LVHW020304271023
762248LV00047B/921

9 781958 89102